THE ACCIDENTAL ADVENTURES OF ONION O'BRIEN

—

THE HEAD OF NED BELLY

THE ACCIDENTAL ADVENTURES OF ONION O'BRIEN

—

THE HEAD OF NED BELLY

JASON BYRNE

ILLUSTRATED BY OISÍN McGANN

GILL BOOKS

Gill Books
Hume Avenue
Park West
Dublin 12
www.gillbooks.ie

Gill Books is an imprint of M.H. Gill & Co.

First published in hardback 2019
This paperback edition published 2020
978 0 7171 8952 6

Designed by Graham Thew
Edited by Oisín McGann
Printed by ScandBook in Lithuania

This book is typeset in Nimrod.
The paper used in this book comes from the wood pulp of managed forests. For every tree felled, at least one tree is planted, thereby renewing natural resources.

A CIP catalogue record for this book is available from the British Library.

5 4 3 2 1

ACKNOWLEDGEMENTS

I'd like to thank everyone who helped me along the way with this book. Gill Books for their amazing support, especially Deirdre Nolan, Catherine Gough, Sarah McCoy, Teresa Daly and Ellen Monnelly.

The amazing Oisín McGann for his beautiful and funny illustrations, and for being by my side at all those tricky children's book festivals.

My wonderful mam and dad, Paddy and Eithne, who have had a huge influence on this book.

My sisters Rachel and Eithne, and brother Eric – they, too, are in this book without really knowing it.

All my old mates who played with me as a child and who taught me, and each other, how to have the best childhood ever in Ballinteer.

The biggest dedication ever EVER goes to my stunning, clever, always loving children. Everything I do, every breath I take, every word I speak or type is for you my beautiful boys, Dev and Dan xx.

Self-portrait by *Devin*   Portrait of Dad by *Daniel Byrne*

CHAPTER ONE:
—
THE BATTLE OF THE BIG LEAK

The four kids were not going to let this happen. The Valley was *their* place. The Big Leak was *their* stream. Onion, Sive, Dallan and Clíona had been coming here since they were slightly younger kids. This wild, rough spot, hidden among the trees, held a special place in their hearts. It was a place away from the grown-ups and their rules. The builders, with all their big machines and plans, were not going to turn it into another boring block of apartments.

This would be a moment that would go down in the history of Ballinlud. It would be an epic battle, like in *The Avengers* or *Star Wars* or . . . *Coronation Street.*

There was a high, grassy bank separating the road from the Valley, the sheltered strip of wasteland that ran along either side of the Big Leak. The builders were going to dig out that bank so they could move their machines in and start laying foundations for the apartment block. Their vehicles were already parked along the side of the road as they waited for the digger driver to plough into the bank that blocked their way.

Sive O'Connor, Dallan Okoye, Clíona O'Hare and Onion O'Brien were the four core members of the gang they called the Five O's. Derek, Onion's older brother, was officially the fifth member, but he always objected to being included, saying he wasn't part of 'their stupid gang'.

The core four Five O's came running along the bank and scrambled down in front of the JCB as its engine started with a rumbling growl. Onion linked arms with Sive, who did the same with Dallan, who hooked his arm into Clíona's.

Together, they faced the digger as the driver peered through his windscreen at them. The foreman, the boss whose head was so big that his hard hat looked like a kid's party hat, turned to stare at them.

'This is it!' Onion said in a shaky voice. 'They're not getting through. Right, guys?'

'Damn right! This is for the Valley!' Sive said, her face set in a determined expression as she chomped down on the gum she always had in her mouth.

'THE DIGGER IS RUBBISH! THE BUILDER IS BAAAAAD! SAVE THE BIG LEAK! WOOOOO AAAAAGH!'

Dallan and Clíona took up the chant. Then Onion, trying his best to remember it, joined in too.

'THE DIGGER IS RUBBISH! THE BUILDER IS BAAAAAD! SAVE THE BIG LEAK! WOOOOO AAAAAGH!'

Over and over they chanted, feeling a little bit braver each time. The builders started coming closer. The four kids chanted louder, looking as defiant as they could.

'Get out of there, ye little guzzers!' the foreman bellowed, striding towards them. 'Go on, get out of it, before one of you gets killed and I have to call yer mammies!'

He sounded really annoyed. The four members of the Five O's fell silent, trembling, but still they stood their ground. The foreman fixed his party-hat helmet and held his belly with both hands. He glared at them, furious, and pulled out his phone.

'That's it,' he said in a low, serious voice. 'If I can't talk sense into you, I'm goin' to have to call . . . *the guards.*'

The way he said it was a bit like a pirate. It sounded like he was telling them they had to

walk . . . *the plank.* Onion looked at his friends, who all looked back at him. This had been Onion's idea. He had led them here. He knew that if he stayed, they'd all stay. Not because he was the leader or anything, but because he was the weakest link in the chain. His nerve was always the first to break. But he swore that wouldn't happen *this* time.

'We're not breaking the law,' Clíona muttered, straightening the headband that framed her long face. 'This is the public part of the road. They can't do anything to us.'

Clíona had looked this up before they came out. She was good at that sort of stuff. Dallan, who was good at talking to grown-ups, looked the foreman in the eye.

'Believe me, gentlemen, we're just the point of the spear. Don't start something that you can't finish,' he said firmly. 'You don't want to bring the guards into this. The best thing would be to just turn around and go on your way. You mess with us, you mess with the whole of Ballinlud!'

The foreman made a show of looking around.

'That's funny, 'cos I don't see the whole of Ballinlud here,' he said, shaking his head. 'I only see four kids with uppity notions. I think I'm just goin' to call . . . *the guards*.'

Using his free hand, Onion pushed his glasses up his nose. They tended to slip down when he was sweaty, and he tended to get sweaty when he was terrified. He had an eyepatch over his left eye because his right eye was wonky. To stop it being lazy, the doctor had decided to cover up the *good* one. This still made no sense to Onion, because he could never get his right eye to do what he wanted, especially when he was under stress.

He was under a lot of stress now. His eye turned in towards his nose and stayed there, ignoring the frantic orders from his brain. His long, thin, white legs felt as if they were made of spaghetti. He felt his chest tighten. Grabbing the inhaler that dangled on a cord around his neck, he took a blast of it, because his lungs didn't work well under stress either. His breathing was coming in little squeaks now.

The foreman had clearly decided that Onion was the easiest target. With big, dramatic movements, he dialled a number on his phone and held it to his ear, his face taking on that distant look you get when you're waiting for a call to connect. He raised his eyebrows and leaned down towards Onion, as if someone had just answered.

'Hello, is that . . . *the guards*?' He gave a smile of satisfaction, and then put on a concerned expression. 'Yes, I have a very serious situation here. A bunch of lunatics are about to attack myself and my crew. If they do, I'm pretty sure it's straight to jail for them, am I right in saying that? What's that? Oh yes, they're armed!'

'Armed? What does that mean? I have two arms, is that bad?' Onion said to the others, his panic rising.

'Oh yes, they have sticks and all sorts,' the foreman continued. 'Please hurry, we're so frightened . . . and there's one boy in particular I need you to take care of.'

The foreman paused and stared down at Onion.

'A ginger kid with glasses and an eyepatch, odd wheezing noises coming out of him,' he said. 'He's a real problem. I think . . . I think you're going to have to bring the *van especially designed for horrible children* for this one. He's the leader.'

'The *van especially designed for horrible children*?' Onion gasped, not sure what he was hearing. He was crumbling, fast.

'Onion, don't . . .' Sive started to say.

'But he said . . .'

'Don't mind what he said! Onion, don't . . .'

Onion's nerve couldn't last a second longer. He turned and ran for it, bolting up the bank, down the other side and sprinting for the trees further along the stream.

'Don't take me away in the *van especially designed for horrible children*!' he howled as he ran.

THE HEAD OF NED BELLY

The others broke formation and came belting after him. The epic Battle of the Big Leak was over . . . And they had lost.

CHAPTER TWO:
—
THE LEGEND OF NED BELLY

Once they'd made it back to the small woods at the other end of the Valley, the four Five O's slowed down to a walk. Nobody said a thing. They were too disappointed in themselves. Behind them, they could hear the sounds of the JCB engine revving up. Was this it, then? Was this the end of the Valley?

By unspoken agreement, they were heading back to Onion's house. Onion lived with his granny and grandad, his little sister Molly and his older brother Derek, the fifth Five O. It was a pretty laid-back house, as Granny Mary and Grandad Paddy had raised their own kids back in the 1980s, when things were a little different.

Parenting was a bit sloppier in those days, when children would be allowed to wander off from a fairly young age. It would just be assumed they'd gone to a friend's house or something. Their mam or dad might start to ask questions if they didn't come back for dinner, but otherwise, as long as they were alive and conscious and didn't need a hospital, there was no cause for concern. Issued with the traditional warning, 'If you break your leg, don't come running to me,' they were held responsible for their own safety, and that was that.

Top 5 Things You Could Get Away With in the '80s

1. Wandering off for miles in all directions like wildebeest migrating across the plains of the housing estates, only to return before dark

2. Punching holes in milk-bottle lids left at people's doorsteps, taking a free drink,

then blaming it on the birds and their beaks

3. Not going to Mass by finding out the priest's name from your mates and making sure not to return home too early in case it was a slow priest, and not everyone's favourite: a speedy-talking priest

4. Taking a Club Milk bar from the bikky cupboard, unwrapping it carefully, removing the bar, folding the wrapping back into its original shape, then placing it back in the bikky cupboard and hey presto! No one knows you ate a chocolate bar before dinner . . . until Grandad tries the same trick

5. Not buying your big brother Derek a birthday present, instead adding 'and Onion' after 'From Granny and Grandad' to the present tag

This complete lack of supervision on their grandparents' part meant Onion and Derek had a lot of freedom. For this reason, their house was the base of operations for the Five O's. Sive, Dallan and Clíona could get away with much more here than they could in their own homes.

You might wonder why Onion, along with his brother and sister, lived with their grandparents instead of their mother and father. The fact of the matter was, their parents had disappeared some years before, in mysterious circumstances.

But that is another story for another time.

Even though Onion and Derek did wonder sometimes, it had nothing to do with Granny Mary and Grandad Paddy being careless parents. Molly, their sister, was only little, and still needed a bit of attention.

Molly was on the floor playing with Lego when Onion and the others trudged in the back door to the kitchen. Granny was doing battle with something covered in fat, boiling the jaypers out of it in a big pot. Even though whatever it was had died long ago, she was struggling to keep it in as the whole thing started to boil over.

Onion wasn't watching where he was going as he came in and he kicked over Molly's creation, which was either a multi-coloured tree, a frozen explosion or a fairy castle. It skated across the floor and smashed against the wall behind Grandad, who was sitting at the table, hidden behind his newspaper as usual. Onion gasped in horror as he saw the Lego creation smash into pieces. Granny put her hand to her mouth and then came the sound of a long, in-drawn breath. Sive hurriedly pulled her hearing aids from her ears. Even Grandad noticed, dropping his paper slightly, his eyes going wide.

Molly let rip with her scream . . .

Top 5 Things That Make Molly Scream

1. Producing a lollipop from your pocket for her

2. Her reflection in anything: the cooker, the window, a mirror . . . even Grandad's glasses, which usually resulted in him screaming back at her in fright

3. Saying clouds aren't marshmallows – she has none of that

4. Granny making popcorn in the pot – she screams at every pop

5. Rubber gloves for the washing-up – no one knows why

Every young child can scream, of course, but few of them had Molly's superpowers. What made her shriek so awful was that she was also sensitive to loud noise. This meant she was scared of her own scream. When she started screaming, she would give herself a fright, which made her want to scream even more, which scared her again, which made her . . . well, you get the idea. Once she'd started into this loop of scare-and-scream, she had to be distracted by something quickly or she'd go into Full Tantrum and nobody wanted that.

Unfortunately, in the panic, everyone tried to distract her at the same time and this just made more noise. She was already getting cranked up and then she went off like a fire alarm that's hit its thumb with a hammer. Everyone cowered away, covering their ears, except for Granny, who dived for the biscuit tin on the counter, yanked it open and held her hand out to Molly.

'MOLLY, D'YA WANT A BIKKY LOVE? HAVE A BIKKY!

MOLLY!

TAKE THE BIKKY, MOLLY!

MOLLY! LOOK AT THE BIKKY! TAKE

THE BIKKY, MOLLY!'

Such was the deafening noise in the kitchen, it took a few moments for the little girl to notice she was being offered the treat. Granny was strict about treats and didn't usually use them as bribes, but this was a broken Lego situation and extreme measures were called for. Molly sobbed shakily, sniffed, and took the biscuit, nibbling it shyly as she watched everyone come out of hiding.

'It's cool, I'm here!' roared Derek as he bounded into the kitchen, late to the action as usual. Derek was everything Onion wasn't: smart, popular, fit, good-looking, blessed with a phone of his own and *definitely* not in Onion's stupid gang, even if he'd once been the fifth Five O. He was too cool for that now.

THUMP!

'Owwwwwwwwwww!' shouted Onion. Derek had given him a full-on dead arm.

'I'll save you, Molly,' said Derek. 'Why did you upset her, Onion?'

Before Onion could defend himself, Derek spotted the biscuits and grabbed one from Granny's hand.

'Ooooh, bikkies!'

'DEREK!' Granny roared, but he had already spun on his heels and disappeared upstairs, quick as lightning.

'That was a bad one, Onion,' Granny said, twisting her hands together. She turned to Molly, hoping her scream bomb had been defused. 'But it's all okay now. And . . . and Clíona will help you fix your . . . your . . . your thing that you made, won't you Clíona?'

Clíona nodded quickly, pulling down her oversized shirt from where it had been covering her head. She was a genius with Lego and always happy to play with it. Molly nodded happily to show she accepted this deal.

Everything was all right again, except that Molly and Derek had gotten a biscuit and Onion hadn't. This didn't seem fair to him. He'd had a rough time too. To add insult to injury, the biscuits were from the tin, not a packet. THE TIN! That's where Granny kept the special occasion biscuits. It was even a chocolate one with the jelly star on top. That was like giving Molly the jewel from the centre of a queen's crown.

Onion thought about screaming to see if he could get a biscuit too, but he thought better of it in case Derek and his knuckles made another appearance. Instead, he told his grandparents about the Valley.

'They've started digging up the Valley,' he said, trying not to cry.

'Had to happen sometime, Onion,' Grandad Paddy said. 'They couldn't leave that bit of wasteland lying around forever. You know it's Mayor Ronald Bump himself who owns it? Not a man to waste money, that fella. Or share it, either. Wouldn't give you the steam off his pee.'

'Paddy, language!' Granny said sharply.

'"Pee" isn't a bad word,' he replied. 'Or are we supposed to pretend that pee doesn't exist and nobody needs to do one ever?'

The kids giggled.

'It's still being rude – and I won't have you saying a bad word about Mayor Bump. He's a good friend of Father Murphy! Still, I'm surprised they're building on that spot, what with the legend an' all that.'

'What legend?' Dallan asked.

Dallan was always keen for a story. He considered himself a performer, a 'raconteur', whatever that was, and more of a grown-up than the others. A handsome lad, he always tried to look his best with his designer glasses and the latest labels, but none of the others took him too seriously, because he talked a lot of guff too.

'Have you never heard the legend of Ned Belly?' Granny asked.

When the Five O's all shook their heads, Grandad groaned and retired back behind his newspaper.

'Well, the story goes that back in the time of Oliver Cromwell,' Granny began, 'when he was travelling around the country doing all his bad deeds, he stopped for dinner at a house that stood beside the stream there . . . What do you call it?'

'The Big Leak,' Sive said. She had put her hearing aids back in now and was unwrapping a fresh stick of chewing gum. 'That's just what we call it. We don't know its real name.'

'Well, there was a big house by the . . . the Big Leak, and not much else around back then, so Cromwell stopped and ordered the owner of the house to make him dinner.'

'Ooooh, Cromwell, we learned about him in school. He was nasty,' said Onion.

'He was indeed, Onion. The owner of the house was a rich old miser named Ned Belly. He hated what Cromwell was doing, so before he served him dinner, he spat in his food.'

'Haha! I did that to Derek's dinner once,' laughed Onion.

There was silence around the room, and then . . .

THUMP!

'Owwwwwww!' screamed Onion, as Derek appeared again out of thin air.

'What did you say?' asked Derek.

'I mean, I coughed on it by accident,' Onion tried to backtrack.

'Shhhhhh,' said Clíona, 'I want to hear the rest of the legend.'

'Anyway,' Granny continued, 'when Cromwell found out, he had Ned's head chopped off. Ned Belly's ghost was said to haunt the house until it was knocked down. Now that it's gone, nobody's sure if the ghost is still around, or what. Even so, when I was a little girl, we stayed away from Ned Belly's stream.'

Onion looked over at Molly in alarm, but she was too stuck into fixing up her Lego to hear Granny's grisly tale.

'Cool!' Sive said.

'We never knew the place was haunted!' Onion said with a mixture of fear and excitement.

'There's supposed to be treasure buried around there somewhere too,' Grandad grunted, turning the page of his paper and shaking the folds out of it. 'He was loaded, was old Ned, but he hardly spent a penny. And it's said that he buried his money before Cromwell chopped his head off. Nobody ever found the treasure after he died. There's a whatsit . . . a rhyme, isn't there, Mary?'

'Oh yes!' Granny said, 'Hand me that book, Onion, *The Ghost Whisperer*, I'm sure I read it in there.'

'Oh great,' said Grandad. 'The last time we had that book out, Granny thought your great-aunt Sarah appeared in the attic. We had to call the priest. Me and him got stuck in the attic for hours because the door closed behind us and your granny couldn't reach the handle. He ended up hearing my confession,' Grandad Paddy moaned on.

Onion got Granny's book off the shelf.

'Yes, here it is,' she said when she finished flicking through the pages.

When Ned was dead, they took his head,
But no one listened when he said,
I'll die before you take my gold,
So keep back now 'cos you've been told,
I curse you all who'd steal what's mine,
You'll search and search and see no sign,
The secret's lost with sly old Ned,
Hidden there in his dead head.

There was a moment of silence when she finished, as the Five O's imagined the scene. The soldiers had killed him without realising he was rich, and only he could have told them where he kept his money.

'Yeah, right! The legend of Ned Belly? More like the makey-uppy story to make grannies buy a book legend,' said Derek, who never believed anything, especially if it was fun.

'The locals all knew he was loaded – he even used to tell them to search for it, to tease them,' Granny added. 'He had a reputation as a practical joker. Nobody ever found it. Some say that was the curse. He let them know it was there on his land somewhere, and his ghost stayed around to laugh at everyone who tried searching for it – and to make sure they never found it.'

'That's awesome,' Onion whispered.

'His body was never found, but Cromwell left his head on a pole,' Grandad said lightly. 'A bit of decoration for the locals. The old hall up by your school was a museum years ago. They used to keep the head there. It was . . . what's the word? . . . Yeah, *mummified*. All dried-up lookin'. Don't know what happened to it after the place closed down.'

'Imagine your head on a stick forever. Do you reckon you could still see? I mean, you'd be dead, but maybe you could still see,' said Onion.

THUMP!

'Owwwwwwwwwwwwww!'

'That one was for free, ye dope,' said Derek.

'This is mad,' Onion said, nursing his dead arm. 'Mayor Bump and those builders are going to dig that whole place up. If there's a curse, what do you think will happen if they get near that gold?'

Sive's eyes narrowed. She brushed her fingertips over her dark, spiked-up hair, as if she was imagining her own head was missing.

'Maybe . . .' she said slowly, '. . . maybe, they could wake up that ghost. Maybe *we* could make that happen.'

And so a dangerous idea was born.

CHAPTER THREE:
—
THE OLD HALL

The following day was a Tuesday, and the end of their mid-term break, so they were heading back to school. Everyone was in a bad mood as they walked down Ballinlud Avenue (except Derek, of course, who was in secondary school and therefore too cool to be in their stupid gang), and they were all blaming Onion.

'Why did you have to run?' Dallan was saying. 'I bet that guy never even called the guards. He was just having us on. I know waffle when I hear it, and he was just tryin' to scare us. And you fell for it, you big curtain cack.'

'How could I take the chance?' Onion protested. 'You heard him. He was telling them to bring the *van especially designed for horrible children!*'

'There's no such thing as the *van especially designed for horrible children!*' Sive snapped at him, throwing her arms up. 'How could you believe that?! Guards aren't allowed to just come and take kids away! It was just a stupid story and you swallowed it!'

'Well, it sounded scary at the time,' Onion muttered, though he wasn't sure they were right. If there was such a thing as a garda van that took kids away, it would make sense to keep it a secret, wouldn't it? It would be like those special operations that soldiers did that they couldn't tell anyone about. Or like the *Men in Black*, who kept the Earth safe from aliens. People who knew these types of secrets were supposed to deny that they existed.

St Hilarius' National School was a very ordinary building in the very ordinary Dublin suburb of Ballinlud. It was big for a primary school, with several hundred pupils, and it was named after a rather funny sounding pope, but really, there was nothing very special about it.

Except for the garda patrol car that sat waiting in the car park that morning, when Onion and his friends walked up.

The Five O's had arrived just in time to see two gardaí walking in the front door. One was Garda Fergus Plunkett, known to the local kids as 'The Ferg'. The Ferg was a bit of a dumb clump. However, his action-fanatic partner, Garda Bridie Judge, was not. Onion started wheezing and went weak at the knees.

'They're here, they're here!' he gasped. 'They've come for us! We're done! We're toast!'

'I'm not sure they could be here for us,' Clíona said reasonably. She always tried to be logical about things. 'We didn't break any laws yesterday . . . Okay, apart from maybe trespassing, and I don't think the guards would start a manhunt for that kind of thing. And the builders don't know we go to school here. I don't think this has anything to do with us.'

'We're doomed!' Onion moaned, ignoring her. 'We'll do hard time. They'll make us shave our heads and get prison tattoos!'

'Nobody's shaving *my* head!' Dallan said, pointing to the head in question. 'Do you know how long it takes to get hair looking this good? If I end up in prison, Mam and Dad will stop my pocket money for sure! I'll have to start buying my shower gel from SuperPrice! It'll be a disaster!'

'What's wrong with SuperPrice, ye snob?' Onion asked. 'Granny does *all* our shopping there.'

'I think Clíona's right. This is not about us,' Sive said, thoughtfully grinding her chewing gum between her teeth. 'But let's not take the chance. We'll just hide until they're gone. They won't be long. Nobody stays in a school longer than they absolutely have to.'

Onion, Clíona, Dallan and Sive hurried down the side of the school, out of sight of the front door, and keeping low against the wall so they wouldn't be seen through the classroom windows. There weren't any obvious places to hide. The hedge and ditch were soaking wet after the rain that morning, so the kids' clothes would get wrecked if they crawled in there. The boiler house was locked, and so were the store rooms next to the gym, where all the outdoor sports equipment was kept. If The Ferg and Garda Judge decided to search the school, they were bound to look in those places anyway. No, they needed somewhere less obvious. Somewhere *nobody* ever went.

The gym and the prefabs were at one back corner of the big school complex. In the other was the old hall that had once been the first St Hilarius' National School, about a hundred years ago. Later, it had been turned into a kind of community hall, when the 'new' school was built, which was still back in the olden days. It had included a sad little museum to celebrate the history of Ballinlud, but that had closed years ago.

Now, it was just used for storing junk, like an attic. Even Mr Oily Doyley hardly went in there. Mr Oily Doyley was the school's caretaker, who smelled so much of engine oil that the kids thought he even used it as hair gel. He always told the kids the place was full of rats, so that tended to keep them away too.

'What if there *are* rats?' Sive asked. She *hated* rats.

'They won't do us any harm,' Clíona said. 'They're intelligent, social creatures that don't bite . . . well, unless you do something to really provoke them.'

'You mean, like breaking into their home?' Dallan asked.

'Let's get on with it!' Onion said to them. 'Before somebody sees us!'

The warped double doors of the hall were locked with a chain and padlock. If you pulled them apart as far as they could go, and got down low, and you were a kid rather than an adult, you could squeeze between them. One by one, Onion, Sive, Dallan and Clíona pulled themselves through, into the dark and dusty space beyond. Standing up, they found themselves in a large room surrounded by stacks of boxes, furniture and all sorts of junk. There was little light in the place. The windows were small and filthy, and let in hardly any of the dim Irish sun.

Moving in away from the doors, Clíona switched on the torch on her phone. She was the only one of the four who had a phone, though it rarely *worked* as a phone, because she was normally trying to change it into something else. She was a bit of an inventor, was Clíona. She wasn't often successful, and yet she never saw that as a reason to stop trying.

There were narrow paths through the tall stacks that disappeared into the gloom. Onion wondered how old some of this stuff was. He saw some of the ancient school desks piled on top of each other, the types with bench seats and the holes for the ink pots. There was an old ride-on lawnmower and a wardrobe and a tall glass case with a wooden frame with a kind of pedestal inside it. He turned around and, in those deep shadows, saw a tall figure towering over him.

It had no head.

Onion let out a strangled, gurgling sound that would have been a scream if his throat had worked properly. He stumbled backwards into Clíona, who fell against a large metal storage cabinet that banged against the wall and then tipped forward, toppling against a stack of desks. As the desks fell over, the cabinet jammed into them, tottering to a stop at a steep angle. Its doors flopped open and a whole load of different-sized balls tumbled out: deflated footballs and basketballs, damaged sliotars and cracked tennis balls.

The desks crashed to the ground then, the cabinet clunking down on top of them, narrowly missing Dallan, who stepped out of the way, only to stand on a sliotar and have his foot slip out from under him. The sliotar shot out and bounced off the wall, then the ceiling, knocking out a chunk of plaster. It hit Sive on the head. She squealed, knocked over a coat stand, ducked out of the way, tripped over Dallan, who was now lying on the floor, and plunged into the accidental ball-pit Clíona's fall had just created. Onion was still staring at the headless figure in front of him. He staggered back and fell over on top of his three friends as they were getting up, knocking the wind out of them.

He finally got out his scream, though it sounded like air leaving a balloon when you pull the top of it tight and let the air squeeze through slowly. As the other three kids scrambled frantically to their feet, they all looked to where he was pointing.

'Oh my God! It's the body of Ned Belly!' Onion whisper-screamed.

'It's a mannequin!' Clíona said, shining her light on it. 'Onion, look! It's just a mannequin!'

And it was – only a dummy like the ones in clothes shops, though it was old, and made from wood and leather rather than plastic. It looked wrecked, the clothes on it ragged, and the shadows gave it a creepy appearance. But once it was lit up, they could see the polished woodgrain surface and the joints. Onion was trembling. It took him a minute to calm down.

'This place is a disaster,' Sive commented. 'It's like all this junk is set up as a booby trap.'

'I wonder where the head is,' Clíona said, gazing at the dummy.

'Actually, I think I've found it here,' Dallan replied, coughing out dust as he recovered from his winding. 'Somebody stuck it in with all the footballs.'

Onion picked up a leathery round shape with hair hanging off it. He looked at it, gagged, and let out such a high-pitched scream that only dogs could hear him. In fact, the gang all froze as they heard a dog barking in the distance.

'Jaypers!' Onion whistle-screamed. He hurled the thing away from him and shuffled backwards, as if trying to escape from it.

'What is it?' Sive asked him. 'Onion, what's going on?'

Clíona shone the beam of her phone's torch in among the shadows cast by the high piles of junk, searching for the thing Onion had just thrown away. There it was, sitting in a clear space, in a faint beam of light from one of the windows. With the dust motes floating around it, it had an almost mystical air. This wasn't some piece of a mannequin.

It was a real human head.

CHAPTER FOUR:
—
THE MATTER OF THE HEAD

Suddenly there came the sound of adult voices, and someone rattled the chain on the doors.

'Who's in there?' a voice demanded. 'What's going on in there?!'

It was Mr Oily Doyley and their principal, Ms Betty Lemon (or Ms Bitter Lemon, as the kids called her, because of her constant sour look).

She was the one shouting, and the kids shuddered when they heard the tone in her voice. She was in extra bitter lemon mode.

'Oh flip!' Onion whimpered.

THE MATTER OF THE HEAD

'Alright, we need to get our stories straight,'
Dallan said quickly. 'Whatever you do, don't–'

The padlock clicked, the chains clinked, the
doors swung open, and light flooded in on them.
Silhouetted in the blinding light of the doorway,
and standing beside Ms Bitter Lemon and Mr Oily
Doyley, was Garda Bridie Judge. She was striking
a menacing-looking martial arts pose, her baton
in her hand. Behind her stood The Ferg. The oaf
was trying to look more mean than nervous, and
not quite managing it.

THE HEAD OF NED BELLY

'You lot,' Ms Bitter Lemon growled. 'Why am I not surprised?'

Onion pointed shakily into the shadows, wading through the footballs in his hurry to get out.

'It's a head!' he wailed. 'It's a real *human head*!'

And suddenly, nobody was looking at the kids anymore.

Now that all signs of danger had passed, The Ferg took charge, much to Ms Bitter Lemon's annoyance. Broad in the body and short in the legs, the red-faced goon had all the bluster of a man who was constantly trying to cover up his lack of intelligence by sounding as official as possible. Garda Judge stood back, looking bored and dangerous. Small, blonde, hard-faced and athletic, Judge was waiting for the moment she could leap into action against some *proper* criminals, preferably some that were heavily armed. She'd been in the guards for years now, and still hadn't had the opportunity to use a spinning kick on anyone. It was starting to grate on her nerves.

The gang of children were trooped back to the principal's office for interrogation. Ms Bitter Lemon casually held the gruesome head in her hand like it was a shopping bag. She was tall and stern, and could have passed for a man or woman, depending on which angle you looked at her. She was also heavily pregnant, a fact that still amazed many of the kids in the school.

Top 5 Things Pupils Believe About Teachers

1. They have no lives outside school

2. They sleep in the school

3. They have their friends over to the school at night

4. They don't have friends, actually, probably just other teachers who live in the school

5. They don't do poos or wees

Ms Bitter Lemon had swollen ankles and a sore back and needed a very soft cushion to sit down on. All of this tended to make her a bit narky, and she was looking forward to her maternity leave. So were most of the kids in the school – and some of the teachers.

It turned out that the guards were not there looking for the Five O's. They'd come to talk to the staff about a master thief who was operating in the area. Known as 'the Jackeen', he was thought to have grown up in Ballinlud, and word on the street was that he was back. Some informants thought that the Jackeen had once been a pupil in St Hilarius' National School, so the guards had come to talk to some of the teachers who'd been working here for years.

However, the discovery of a human head in the old school hall had now distracted the guards from their original line of inquiry. Ms Bitter Lemon had plonked it on her desk, next to a tin of biscuits, her 'World's Best Teacher' mug and a book entitled *So,*

You're Having Your First Baby. Her face seemed extra sour as she examined it closely.

The head looked like somebody had folded human features into the loose skin of a brown leather ball, and then pasted some bristly, brittle black hair over the top, back and sides. The four kids all sat on a bench against one wall of her office, staring at the creepy thing.

' . . . I'm going to ask you one more time,' The Ferg said for the seventh time. 'What were you doing in that building? How did you come to be in possession of that head? It's a valuable . . . eh . . . eh . . . antique, and it's probably worth a lot of money.'

'I don't think you can call a *human head* an antique,' Clíona interrupted.

'I think she's right,' Ms Bitter Lemon said, nodding.

'Whatever!' The Ferg gestured in irritation. 'Maybe you four are working for the Jackeen, eh? Is that it? Are you working for the Jackeen?'

Garda Judge tutted and rolled her eyes in disgust.

'Oh for God's sake, Fergus, they're just kids! They're nobodies!'

'That's harsh,' Onion said, and took a blast of his inhaler to ease his tight chest.

'We keep telling you,' Dallan replied, exasperated. He was doing most of the talking. He normally did when fast-talking guff was needed. 'We thought we heard a *cat* in there, and it sounded like it was stuck or something. We just wanted to help a *cat*. Is that so wrong?'

'Do you really expect me to believe you went looking for a cat and found a human head instead?' The Ferg snorted. 'There's something else going on here! What kind of fool do you take me for?'

'We refuse to answer that question on the grounds that it might incriminate us,' Dallan replied.

'All right, that's enough! Guards, I think I can handle things from here on in. There's no need to make a drama out of this,' Ms Bitter Lemon told The Ferg and Garda Judge, as she leaned back in her big swivel chair. 'It's nothing to do with this criminal of yours. It's the head of Ned Belly. I visited the museum when I was young, back when it was still open. The head was on display in a glass case. Scared the willies out of me at the time. I heard it had disappeared when the museum was closed down, that it had been stolen. Obviously, someone just mislaid it.'

'We should take it in for testing,' The Ferg said.

'Testing for *what*?' Ms Bitter Lemon said, with a quizzical expression. 'It's a museum exhibit, not evidence in a crime. We'll hand it over to Mayor Bump and the council, and they can decide what to do with it. Now, if you're quite finished here, these children need to get back to their class, and I've work to be getting on with. But thank you for your help.'

The Ferg looked offended that he'd just been dismissed, while Garda Judge appeared relieved to be on the move again. The children watched them go, the tension easing slightly as the door closed behind them. Then Ms Bitter Lemon sat up straighter, grunting as she got a twinge in her back. She turned her attention to her pupils.

'As for *you* four delinquents,' she began, her 'Targets Locked' tone activated, 'I've just one thing to say to you . . .'

Her voice drifted off. She suddenly got a funny look in her eyes. She grimaced, groaned and cupped both hands under her belly.

'I think I'm having my baby,' she said.

CHAPTER FIVE:

— FAKING A GHOST

After Ms Bitter Lemon's husband had shown up to take her to the hospital, the school was buzzing with excitement. As it was generally believed by the students that teachers didn't have lives outside school, their principal's pregnancy was very weird altogether. The impending birth, however, seemed to prove that she wasn't faking it, that she was indeed pregnant, that she had a husband and that she didn't actually live in her school office.

Once the pupils had made the necessary adjustments to their world views, they all thought it was pretty cool that one of their teachers was having a baby, even if it *was* a pity the poor child would grow up with a teacher as a mother. No doubt their days would be filled with homework.

At break time, the Five O's got together to discuss their eventful morning. They were all desperately disappointed that they'd failed to stop the builders breaking through into the Valley, but the whole episode with Ned Belly's head had provided a much-needed boost to their spirits. It might have been skin-crawlingly creepy, but it was also utterly cool. Sive was worked up about something now, and as soon as she could get her friends on their own, she shared her idea.

'We could use the ghost!' she told them. 'If we could make the builders believe that the headless ghost of Ned Belly was haunting the site, it might scare them away!'

'That's not going to work,' Clíona said. 'Ghosts aren't real.'

'Who says ghosts aren't real?' Onion asked.

'Science,' Clíona replied.

'We can't make a real ghost anyway,' Dallan said. 'But maybe we could *fake* a ghost. Sive's right. We just need to make it convincing enough. How do we make them believe? We might need some help on this. Who knows the most about ghosts?'

There was a moment's pause.

'Youssef,' the others replied together.

Youssef was the school's expert on all things horror, including films, games, books, comics and spooky stories. He was a great fella to have in your class.

Youssef ran a consultancy service, advising people on the best scares. He was a bit like a kid version of one of those guidance counsellors who helps you figure out what career you should have, except he helped you figure out the best way to scare yourself witless.

He also told fortunes using football cards, for which he charged fifty cents a go in the mall, the space where all the corridors met in the school.

His predictions tended to be ridiculous, but that didn't stop some of them from coming true.

Some fortune-tellers might say vague things like 'You're going to meet someone tall, dark and handsome', or 'You're going on a trip over water'. Youssef would tell you your cat was a secret agent working for an alien race and its job was to watch people typing out their passwords. Once the cats had enough passwords, the aliens were going to take over the internet. Youssef had assured his friends that he had already seen this happening, and some of the kids who had experience of cats believed he might be right.

When the Five O's found him, he was in the resource room doing another reading of the football cards. He had cerebral palsy, and was saving his money to help upgrade his normal wheelchair to a motorised one. When he was finished his reading, the other child left, looking a little pale, and Onion sat down in front of him.

'I need some advice, Yous,' he said. 'How do we fake a ghost?'

'My time ain't cheap,' Youssef told him, trying to look shrewd, despite his round, babyish face. 'If you want help, you gotta pay for a reading.'

Onion sighed and put fifty cents on the table.

'I don't need a reading. I just want to fake a haunting.'

'Let's just see what the cards say,' Youssef said, and dealt out three. A Liverpool striker, a Watford defender and a goalie who'd never got off the bench at Sheffield Wednesday. 'Hmm. That's interesting. *Very* interesting.'

'Fortune-telling isn't a real thing,' Clíona objected.

'What do the cards say?' Dallan asked.

'We just need to learn about *ghosts*,' Sive insisted, rolling her eyes.

Youssef held up his hand to silence them and shifted his wheelchair closer to the table.

'Hush! The cards are speaking to me.'

'Is it football commentary?' Clíona said sceptically.

'This is a time of great danger for you,' Youssef told Onion, ignoring the sceptic. 'I see a decapitated human head . . .'

'*Everybody* knows about that already,' Sive said, rolling her eyes again. Rolling her eyes and chewing gum were Sive's favourite things. 'Everyone knows we found Ned Belly's head.'

'. . . I see a man made of mud. I see Onion in darkness, caught in a spotlight. I see a man with two faces. I hear Onion's sister screaming . . .'

'That could be *any* time,' Onion pointed out.

'. . . I see a wooden puppet. I see a car chase that isn't a car chase. I see . . . *destruction.*'

'Destruction, car chases, wooden puppets?' Onion said in a fearful voice. 'Whatever happened to "you'll come into a great fortune" or all that?'

'Well, you won't,' Youssef said, putting the cards away. 'It's mud men and darkness for you, mate. Sorry.'

'A wooden puppet,' Clíona said, almost to herself, lost in thought. 'A *puppet.*'

'You thinking what I'm thinking?' Dallan asked, a sly smile spreading over his face, dangling his fingers as if he was hanging something from them.

'Yeeeaaaaah . . .' Clíona said.

'What?' Onion asked.

'Yeah, what?' Sive asked too.

Clíona motioned them out of the room. They found a quiet spot in the hallway.

'I know how to make our ghost,' she said softly. 'But we have to go back into the old hall.

And we're going to have to do it at night, without anyone seeing us. We need to borrow something.'

'No way,' Onion whimpered, his head shaking vigorously. 'Absolutely no way. No darkness. No "borrowing". Nope, nope, nope. In case you've forgotten, the last time we went in there, we found a *dead head* and the *guards* caught us and now there's a criminal on the loose somewhere out there too. God knows what else is in that hall . . . hiding in the dark.'

'Onion,' Sive said. 'Do you want to save the Valley or not?'

They had him with that. He still felt the shame of letting them down once already. He couldn't do that again. No, whatever it took, they had to get the builders out of the Valley.

'Okay. Okay then,' he said, feeling a shudder running through his body. 'What have you got in mind?'

CHAPTER SIX:

—

LAYING PLANS

After school, they all went back to Onion's house. Grandad was at some job somewhere. Even though he was old enough to retire, he worked as a handyman for a few different places. Granny and Molly were on the sofa in the sitting room, watching a video of Barney the Dinosaur. This was an actual video *tape*, in an actual video-tape recorder, because Granny and Grandad had set up the house the way they wanted back in the 1980s and had pretty much kept it that way ever since.

There was no wi-fi because there was no modem in the house. There wasn't even a working computer – unless you counted the antique in a box in the attic that needed *cassette tapes* to play games on. Grandad didn't like having anything in the house that he couldn't fix, and the list of what he couldn't fix was getting shorter with age. Onion lived in terror of their boxy old TV failing one day, because Grandad didn't trust those flat-screen ones. He said they looked too thin to be healthy.

Top 5 Things Grandad Thinks Are Too Thin to Be Healthy

1. TV screens

2. Biscuits, especially Rich Tea

3. Blankets and duvets – sure there's no heat in them anymore

4. Toilet seats – the big wooden seats were great, loads of room for your bum

5. His wallet

The four members of the Five O's went out to the back garden and down to the shed at the end.

Clíona and Dallan were running the show, having concocted the plan. The gang was going to need torches, ropes, some other bits and pieces, and a way to open the chain on the door of the old hall. They were discussing this, looking through Grandad's tools, when a voice piped up from the open shed door, making them jump.

'Whatcha doin'?'

It was Molly, standing there all innocent and freckly looking, one hand playing with her frizzy red hair. She was not alone . . .

'Yeah, whatcha doin'?' repeated Derek in a Molly voice. They hadn't heard him arrive home from the secondary school.

Onion was holding a hacksaw in his hand. He quickly hid it behind his back.

'We're just getting ready to do some jobs,' he said.

'I love jobs! Can I help?' said Molly.

'No, you're too young,' said Onion.

'I am *not* too young!' Like any child, Molly was outraged at the thought that there was anything she was too young for. 'I help Granny with washing the clothes!'

This help normally involved standing beside the washing machine and taking everyone's clothes from the laundry pile and trying them on, with Granny pulling them off her so she could put them in the machine. This was the kind of help Onion could do without.

'I'll help instead if you don't tell me what you're doing.' Derek grabbed Onion by a fistful of his jumper and pulled him close to his face. They were nose to nose. 'Your eye's gone funny.'

'No, it's not,' Onion replied.

'It is. It's going extra wonky there.'

Onion's wonky eye was always betraying him. Any time he tried to lie, his eye turned in, as if it were pointing at his nose, as if saying, 'Look, look, his nose is getting longer. Look at the liar's big nose!' It was so unfair, having an eye that would squeal on you.

Top 5 Reasons for Onion's Eye to Go Extra Wonky

1. Lying

2. Farting – amazing talent, this

3. When his alarm went off in the morning

4. Sneezing or coughing

5. If he got too close to electrical sockets

'Hey there, Molly!' Dallan said in a bright voice, brushing past Onion. 'Remember that time you were collecting worms in a jar? Did you find any more?'

'Nah. Worms are so *yesterday*,' Molly snorted. 'I gave them to Jordan down the street. He eats them. Now I'm collecting nettles.'

'That's brilliant! Why don't you show me your nettles, eh?'

'Hang on, Molly, let's see what this lot are really up to,' said Derek.

'Derek! Derek!' One of Derek's mates had jumped up on the wall and was calling him over.

Derek dropped everything and ran over, but not before giving Onion a dead arm.

THUMP!

'Owwwwwwwwwww!' Onion took the pain. It was worth it to be rid of Derek.

Dallan had finally persuaded Molly to show him her nettles and they headed off too.

With Molly distracted, Onion, Sive and Clíona finished gathering what they needed. They bundled it into a heavy-duty plastic bag, closed up the shed, and headed back to the room Onion shared with Derek.

With the door safely closed, they all took deep breaths of relief and Onion dropped the bag on the floor. He held his hands out to the others to urge them to be quiet, and went to listen at the door, to make sure they wouldn't be disturbed.

'Lift those legs! Tense that tum! Do it all together or you'll get a fat bum!' a voice called out of nowhere.

They all jumped with fright, but then Clíona fumbled for her pocket.

'Lift those legs! Tense that tum! Do it all together or you'll get a fat bum!' the voice said again.

'Sorry, sorry,' she said, pulling out her phone. 'I've got a FitChipper. It measures my steps. I have to do 20,000 steps a day or it nags me until I do. Sorry, I should have muted it.'

'Why do you need a FitChipper?' Onion asked. 'You're a kid, and you're skinny as a rake. We walk *everywhere.*'

'Technology can improve every aspect of our lives,' she retorted, looking hurt. 'So what if I want to be fitter?'

'Yeah, leave her alone,' Sive said, chewing on her gum. 'Come on, let's work out our plan here.'

They laid out everything they had on the floor. There was a coil of rope, some clothes, one of the sheets Grandad used for covering stuff up when he was painting, a hacksaw, a crowbar, a few old torches, some red spray-paint, a screwdriver and some screws.

'This is going to work,' Sive said, nodding.

'*What's* going to work?'

They all spun around. Derek was standing there. They hadn't heard him open the door. He must have come back for something he forgot. He reached for his phone, his hand moving on reflex, and took a photo of the three of them with all their odds and ends. He sneered at them.

'What's all this then? It looks like you just mugged a scarecrow. I knew you were up to something in the shed.'

'It's none of your business!' Onion snapped back at him. 'Get out and leave us alone!'

'This is *my room*, Pox Socks,' Derek said. 'Tell me what's going on. And don't try to lie about it. Your eye's trying to burrow sideways through your head. You've got ten seconds before I post this photo online.'

'No!' Onion cried. 'No, you can't do that. Okay, okay . . . Look . . . We're trying to set up something that will scare the builders working down in the Valley. We want them to believe that the place is haunted by Ned Belly, so they'll stop working down there. Okay?'

Derek's face had a fight with itself. His teenage nature wanted to take the mickey out of his younger brother's comical efforts, but a deeper, more innocent part of him recalled his own fond memories of the Valley. It was a sacred place for the kids of Ballinlud. After a few different expressions crossed his features, he softened and shook his head.

'Ah, look,' he said. 'Onion . . . Look, I know how you feel, but this thing's a done deal. Ronald Bump owns that land and he's gonna do whatever he wants with it. This is the real world. Kids can't change this kind of thing. D'ye really think you can scare grown men away with a makey-uppy ghost? Just let it go.'

It was clear he hated saying it. Derek didn't want to let it go either, but he was thirteen years old now. He was more sensible and knew the real world was hard and cruel.

'Now get out of here. I need to do my homework. I can't concentrate downstairs with Molly and Dallan goin' on about her nettle collection.'

LAYING PLANS

Derek looked surprised when the younger kids obeyed without any protesting. They'd been all psyched up for their operation and he'd brought their hopes crashing down with his hard reality. Onion, however, was not ready to give up yet.

'You're wrong, you know,' he said to his brother before he left the room. 'We can stop this. We can make a difference. We could really use your help, Derek. You're still one of the Five O's.'

'Just give it up, Onion,' Derek sighed. 'And for the last flippin' time, I'm not in your stupid gang!'

CHAPTER SEVEN:

—

THE MISSION

Desperate times called for desperate measures. Some might even say 'stupid' measures. A few very perceptive people might actually call these particular measures 'bonkers' . . . but that was what these desperate times called for.

It was dusk. The light was fading from the cloudy grey sky. The four Five O's had regrouped and returned to the school, hiding in the hedge that offered a view of the back of the main building and the old hall. It was late enough that no one was there, not even Mr Oily Doyley.

THE MISSION

Their goal was to steal the mannequin that they'd seen in the hall that morning. They were going to use it to make a ghost puppet and scare the builders away from the Valley. They were aware that what they were doing was 'breaking and entering' and technically 'stealing'. Clíona had explained that this qualified as 'burglary', but they reasoned that it was for a good cause – saving the Valley. Besides, they were going to return the mannequin as soon as they were finished with it. They huddled there in silence. Then:

'Lift those legs! Tense that tum! Do it all together or you'll get a fat bum!' a voice called out from nowhere, making them jump.

'Sorry, sorry. That's my FitChipper again,' Clíona said, muting the band on her wrist.

'Holy freakin' bejeebus!' Onion squeaked. 'That thing nearly gave me a heart attack!'

'If that thing goes off again,' Sive growled, 'I'm throwing it down the nearest toilet, whether it's been flushed or not.'

They took another minute to calm their pounding hearts. Then it was time to move. Dallan was about to start forward but Sive caught his arm.

'What was that?' she said in a hushed voice.

'What?' Onion asked.

'I thought I saw a light in that window upstairs. Didn't you see it?'

They all stared at the hall. It was a two-storey red-brick building, nearly as big as the gym, with tall, narrow windows downstairs and smaller square ones upstairs, for the smaller, attic-like space. The roof was missing tiles and there must have been a fireplace at one point, because there was a chimney at the near end. Nobody saw any lights in the windows.

'Maybe it was just a reflection,' Clíona suggested.

'Yeah, maybe . . .' Sive muttered.

Dallan hurried forward and the others followed, scurrying across the yard to the double doors of the hall. Instead of trying to open the chain, Clíona had decided to unscrew the brackets the chain ran through, and then she'd screw them back on afterwards. Screwdriver in hand, she reached for the chain. The lock came open in her hands, the ends of the chain falling loose.

'Wow! How did you do that?' Onion asked.

'I *didn't*,' Clíona said in a low voice, an uneasy look on her face. 'It was already open.'

'Oily Doyley must have forgotten to lock it,' Dallan said.

'But it was hanging in one piece,' Sive said. 'It *looked* like it was locked. Somebody must have opened the padlock and left it hooked on like that.'

'That's how he forgot,' Dallan insisted. 'Because it looked locked.'

Nobody was entirely happy with this explanation, but it did mean the door was open and they didn't have to break in, which had to be a good thing. Now they just needed to find the mannequin.

Clíona stood just inside the door to keep watch while the others sought out the dummy. They turned on the torches, aiming them low, and split up to start looking. It looked like Mr Oily Doyley had tidied up the mess they'd made, but the mannequin wasn't hard to find. Onion didn't even get a fright this time when the beam of his torch fell upon the headless figure, standing up beside a grandfather clock.

They'd been hoping to take it apart so that they could carry it in two separate bags, but they couldn't find any obvious way to disassemble it. They were going to have to carry it as it was. Sive and Dallan got either side of it, putting its arms over their shoulders, and then they lifted its thighs, so they could carry it in a kind of sitting position. Its feet were attached to a stand, which was heavy and knocked against their shins when they tried to walk.

'Okay, let's go, let's go,' Onion said, a tremor in his voice. 'This place is creeping me out.'

Onion shone his torch ahead of them so they wouldn't trip up on anything. They were just about to start forward when they heard the sounds of someone moving upstairs. They froze. There was no mistaking it. Slow, soft footsteps that they might never have heard if the old floorboards didn't squeak as much as they did. The noise struck terror into them. If the person came downstairs, they'd catch the Five O's (all except Derek, who still insisted he wasn't in their stupid gang).

If they ran, they might be spotted through the upstairs windows. Maybe they'd already been seen coming into the building.

Onion started wheezing and took a suck of his inhaler.

'I told you I saw a flumpin' light!' Sive said in a scared growl.

'This is not the time!' Dallan whispered back. 'What are we going to do?'

'Who is it?' Onion asked. 'Is it Oily Doyley? Why hasn't he got the lights on?'

That made them stop and think. Why *didn't* the other person have the lights on? Onion recalled the way the padlock had been opened and left hanging to look as if it was still locked. Like leaving the lights off, that was the act of a person who didn't want anyone else knowing they were there. The kind of person who could open a padlock without leaving a mark on it, without needing a key.

'D'you . . . d'you think that *they've* broken in too?' he said in a bewildered voice. 'Like . . . like . . . an actual *burglar*?'

'But what are they here for?' Dallan said. 'This stuff is all junk, it's worthless.'

'How about we stop talking about it and get out of here!' Sive hissed. 'If they're a burglar, then we're *witnesses*. What d'you think they might do to us if they find us here? We have to move! Now!'

'But they'll see us through the windows if we run!' Onion retorted, pointing up at the ceiling.

'It doesn't matter,' she said. 'If they've broken in too, who are they going to tell? But if they catch us here – and we see who it is . . . Come on, let's *go*!'

Clíona was coming towards them, gesturing towards the sounds upstairs. They nearly charged through her, still carrying the mannequin. They dragged her along with them, out the double doors, making no attempt to close them afterwards. Luckily, there was still no one around outside. The

THE HEAD OF NED BELLY

Five O's rushed across the schoolyard. Onion had to stop for a moment, bending over to catch his breath, which he'd lost due to a severe case of panic.

Straightening up, he felt an insane urge to look up at the first-floor windows of the old hall. Don't look, he told himself. You *really* don't want to look. Why would you look? So, of course . . . he looked.

And through the glass of one small window, filthy with grime and dust, he saw a vague shape. A pale, odd face, shaped like a monkey nut, with piercing eyes that peered out from under a deep brow.

It stared straight at him.

Onion's wonky eye went haywire. He wheezed in as much air as his deflated lungs could take and he let out a long wail. Then he turned and started running. The others were surprised to see him fly past them – Onion was normally the *slowest* runner in the gang – and he didn't even stop for the ditch. He leapt over it and through the gap in the hedge that led out into the green beyond.

Even then, Onion didn't stop. His legs carried him home at a frantic pace that got him as far as his front garden, where he collapsed face-first on the grass and lay wheezing until his friends caught up with him.

They were all relieved that they'd got out without being caught, and were feeling a bit hyper as they carried the mannequin and Onion into the back garden and down to the shed where they'd agreed to hide it. They didn't make much of Onion freaking out – hardly a week went by without him freaking out about something, and this had been a pretty dramatic evening, all things considered.

When he'd regained his senses a bit, Onion left his friends to their chatter and staggered up to the kitchen. He needed a glass of milk to calm his nerves. The rest of his family weren't there, thankfully, though Grandad's paper was lying on the table. As he drank back his milk, Onion's gaze fell on the open page. One particular photo caught his attention. The caption said it was the only known image of the master criminal, the Jackeen.

Onion nearly choked on his drink. The figure was tall, thin, muscular, with hair in a slicked-back widow's peak, a white, clean-shaven, monkey-nut-shaped face and piercing eyes. It was the same man he'd seen through the window of the old hall only minutes before. He had seen the face of the Jackeen.

And the Jackeen had seen his.

CHAPTER EIGHT:
THE NEW TEACHER

Onion was still shaken up when he came into school the following morning. It was a Wednesday. They were supposed to be carrying out their operation against the builders that afternoon, but he didn't think his nerves could take any more strain. He'd suggested to his friends that they hold off for a few days, but Sive told him that the longer they had the mannequin, the more likely it was that someone would notice it was missing. They had to go ahead with it as soon as possible.

The four kids arrived into their classroom to find Mrs Talcum, their teacher, standing with a tall, very wide man that none of them recognised. The man had a narrow face, half hidden behind round, thick-framed glasses and a bushy, drooping moustache over a large nose. His skin was almost white. His hair was black and slicked back. He wore a black suit and looked more like an undertaker than a teacher. He had a protruding bum that you could have probably stood on if you were trying to reach something on the top shelf.

'Children, this is Mr Brody,' Mrs Talcum said to them. 'The . . . sudden arrival of Ms Lemon's new baby means she's had to go on leave earlier than we'd expected. Because I'm vice-principal, I have to fill in for Ms Lemon until she comes back. Thankfully, Mr Brody was able to stand in on short notice. He'll be taking you for the next couple of weeks. I'm sure you'll be on your *best behaviour* for him.'

They heard her warning tone. Mrs Talcum didn't use the words 'substitute teacher', although that was what Brody was. The teachers of St Hilarius' considered this particular class a 'bit of a handful', not because they were a bunch of messers – though they were – and not because it was a challenge to keep their attention on anything – though it was – but because of the *mix*.

Sometimes, in a class, you got a dodgy mix. This was one such class. In this case, it was a combination of head-the-balls, pointless rebels and back-chatty smart-alecs. They weren't *bad*, they were just . . . chaotic. Whatever it was about the specific chemistry of personalities in this class, they were exhausting to teach for any but the most elite teachers like Mrs Talcum. Feeding a substitute teacher to a class like this was the equivalent of sending a cow to wade through a river full of piranhas.

Top 5 Things Teachers Need to Get Through a School Day

1. Special grown-up tea in a mug

2. Hope

3. Sarcasm

4. A good scream in the staff toilets

5. Biscuits

All eyes turned to the new teacher, measuring him up, as these young minds tried to assess what they were dealing with. He looked too old to be one of those student teachers starting in a school for the first time, though not quite so old that he was doddery. They thought he was in his

thirties, maybe. He wasn't smiling or trying to appear kind. He looked like he didn't know how. The children immediately guessed that Mr Brody was not the type to let kids run riot, as some inexperienced substitute teachers might do.

'Mr Brody,' Mrs Talcum said, 'I leave them in your capable hands.'

And with that, she left. Brody walked sideways, awkwardly sliding himself between the whiteboard and the teacher's desk. He turned to look at the board. As he did this, his protruding bum swiped the whole teacher's desk clean, sending papers, books, Sellotape and all sorts of stationery to the ground.

The class laughed . . .

'QUIET!' roared the new teacher.

The class fell silent as they watched Mr Brody try to pick up the items he had knocked over. He seemed to find it very hard to bend over. He had to kind of lean sideways while holding onto the desk at the same time. As he did this, a weird noise started to come from . . . somewhere. It was a low barping noise, as if air was being let out of a blow-up bed . . . and it happened every time Mr Brody tried to pick up something.

BAAAAAAAAARRRRRRRRP . . .

The whole class were struggling to hold the laughter in. Sweat began to appear on the pupils' heads. They couldn't keep this up. It was torture.

BAAAAAAAAARRRRRRRRP . . .

Every so often, Mr Brody would look up and stare at the kids with his beady eyes. They didn't dare laugh, even though the faster he bent over, the quicker the barps escaped from him.

BAAAAAAAAARRRRRRRRP . . .

Onion was having a slow heart attack along with everyone else. Smirks and small amounts of laughter were leaking out of the kids' faces. Where was this noise coming from? It didn't seem to be a fart. Finally, everything was back on the desk. Onion and the class could relax . . . for now.

'We shall start with some mathematics,' he said in a bored voice. 'Have you done much algebra?'

There were puzzled expressions as some of the kids exchanged glances, wondering what he was talking about.

'What's an Algie Bra?' Onion asked Clíona, who was sitting next to him. 'Is that for measuring boob sizes?'

'No,' Clíona said in a firm but quiet voice. She called out to the teacher. 'Mr Brody, we haven't done algebra yet . . . Well, *I* do it, but that's just for a bit of fun at home. We haven't done any in school.'

'What about calculus?' Mr Brody asked, looking irritated.

'Sir . . . if . . . if we haven't done algebra, we *definitely* haven't done calculus,' Clíona said. In a timid voice, she added, 'Mr Brody, this is a *primary* school.'

'What are they teaching children these days?' their new teacher inquired. 'What about science? Have you covered Newton's Three Laws of Motion yet? Or any nuclear theory?'

'No, sir,' Onion answered, looking as bewildered as everyone else. 'Sir, we're doing stuff like . . . y'know . . . multiplication and . . . and division and stuff? And, like, for science, we're doing bits of the body and . . . and types of food an' all that?'

'Your knowledge of science is almost as bad as your grasp of English, young man!' Mr Brody declared. 'It seems we have a lot of work ahead of us. Very well, we shall begin with some basic English grammar. Now, can anyone give me the definition of a "fronted adverbial"?'

This time, even Clíona didn't have a clue what he was talking about.

Mr Brody seemed to know a lot about a lot of things, and yet he didn't seem to have any knowledge of what ten- and eleven-year-olds were supposed to know, or how to explain things to them. This was odd, considering he was a *teacher.* It had never occurred to the children before, but they were beginning to suspect that teaching involved more than just standing at the top of the class saying things. Perhaps teachers had to *think* about what they were going to say before they walked into a class. Perhaps they even had to have *plans.*

Mr Brody clearly did not.

The more Onion looked at his new teacher, the more something started to bother him. He couldn't pin it down, but there was something very disturbing about Mr Brody. It wasn't his narrow head or his hair in a slicked-back widow's peak, or the way it was perched on a really wide body in that black suit and white shirt. It wasn't his big, thick-framed glasses, or the huge nose and the droopy moustache, or even the odd BARP noise, and yet it was *all* of that. Something about the whole look just didn't fit together.

Later on that morning, their new teacher had started to explain the chemical formula for cement. The children were still trying to write out examples of the 'future perfect continuous tense'. Mr Brody noticed that some of the students had just given up and put their heads down on their desks. Others were sitting with their eyes glazed over while a few had broken down crying. He took off his glasses for a moment and pinched the bridge of his nose.

It took Onion a few seconds to notice that Mr Brody's face wasn't just narrow. It was kind of a monkey-nut shape, with a deep brow and big jaw and caved-in cheeks. He noticed his eyes, without the glasses, just before Mr Brody put them back on. There was no mistaking that deep-sunk gaze beneath the heavy brow.

It was the same face he'd seen at the window last night, and in the newspaper. *He was looking into the face of the Jackeen.*

Onion took a shot of his inhaler, slid down as low as he could in his chair, and leaned his face on his hand, to hide it as much as he could from the teacher. Clíona noticed that he was trembling and, in a whisper, asked him what was wrong. He didn't answer. He knew if he tried to speak, it would just come out as a raspy wheeze and everyone would notice, including Mr Brody.

When the bell went for lunch, Onion felt as if he'd been holding his breath the whole time. He sucked in air as Mr Brody walked out of the room and headed for the staff room. The other children flowed from the room in their usual rush, lunches in hand.

Onion used his sleeve to wipe the coating of sweat from his face and lurched out after his friends, his knees threatening to buckle underneath him.

CHAPTER NINE:
—
AN ANNOUNCEMENT

I never thought I'd say this,' Clíona said as they walked out to the yard, 'but I wish our teacher would stop treating us like we were smart.'

'We're smart enough!' Sive objected. 'At least for normal school. *That* was not normal school. That was . . . something else. I think Mr Brody might be a really clever guy who just can't teach.'

'He's the Jackeen!' Onion gasped. 'Mr Brody is the Jackeen! That's the same face I saw in the window of the hall yesterday!'

'Ah, come on, Onion,' Sive sighed, rolling her eyes. 'You're just thinking that because you're still a bit shook after pulling off that job. We all saw the picture in the paper. Mr Brody doesn't look anything like the Jackeen.'

Onion had told them all about the face he'd seen the evening before, of course, and had shown them the picture in Grandad's newspaper. They hadn't been sure whether to believe him or not. Now they clearly thought he was doubling down to try and freak them out too.

'Yeah, Mr Brody is *wide* and the Jackeen is *not* wide,' Dallan said. 'He's a rake. You could fit two Jackeens into one Mr Brody.'

'Mr Brody wears glasses and has a moustache,' Clíona pointed out. 'The Jackeen has neither glasses nor a moustache, Onion. It's just your imagination messing with you.'

'Maybe it's a disguise,' Onion said weakly.

'Why, though?' Sive asked. 'This isn't some show on the telly. Why would he disguise himself so that he could come to a *school*, Onion? Who would do that? Ask yourself. Who would go to *school* if someone wasn't *making* them go to school? How mad would that be?'

It did seem mad when she said it like that. And yet Onion was sure of what he'd seen. They didn't believe him, and he didn't have the strength to argue. He'd hardly slept the night before after the fright of recognising the master criminal in the newspaper and realising the Jackeen might already know who *he* was. It had left him feeling wrecked.

When the children went back to class after lunch, they were told everyone had to go to the assembly hall. Once there, the pupils swarmed into their usual places, with all the junior infants sitting on pads on the floor at the front, and sixth classes standing at the back. A few rows from the back wall, Onion stood with his friends as they waited to find out what was going on. Mrs Talcum said a quick hello and then, to their surprise, introduced an important visitor, Mayor Ronald Bump. He had a small gang of assistants and PR people with him.

AN ANNOUNCEMENT

Mayor Bump was a very rich man who managed to make the best designer suits look sleazy. Tall and stocky, he had a smarmy, bearded face and gelled-back hair with a streak of grey through it. He was always smiling like he'd won something. 'I've won at life,' he'd say, to anyone who'd listen. And if people didn't listen, he'd buy a radio station so that more people would.

He'd got himself elected mayor of Ballinlud because the council tried to stop him cutting down some hundred-year-old trees to build his massive house. Now the trees were gone, his huge house was built, and Ronald Bump had decided that being mayor was great craic altogether. He loved the flashy gold chain he got to wear, which was even bigger

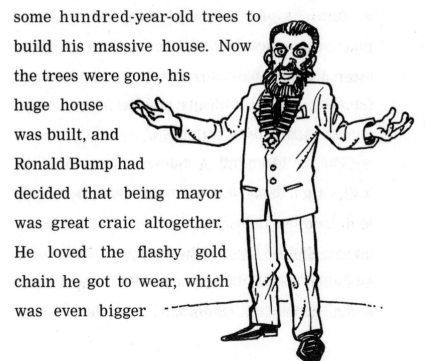

than some of the medallions he liked to drape over his bare, hairy chest when he was dressed casually.

'Girls and boys, I used to be a boy, but I turned into a great man!'

The children and teachers looked on in silence. It was as if Mayor Bump was expecting a round of applause for everything he said.

'I have great news,' he continued, in the voice of someone who'd sell you a sick cow if you let him. 'As part of the building project we're undertaking nearby, we're going to be knocking down that old hall of yours to build you some fantastic new classrooms and get rid of those nasty old prefabs out the back.'

The children all wondered what could be 'fantastic' about a classroom, but they were willing to hear him out.

'As you'll know, the head of Ned Belly, Ballinlud's most famous resident, until I came along, of course.' He laughed to himself as he said this. Only his entourage laughed back. 'Wow, tough crowd. Anyway, the head was finally found yesterday. To mark the occasion, I'm announcing a new competition, the very first *Ballinlud's Got Talent*, to take place this Saturday night. I want to search for some young stars in the hope that we'll find someone who'll one day be as famous as Ned Belly and me!'

'But maybe without getting their head chopped off,' Dallan muttered. Onion had to cover his mouth to muffle his giggles.

'We're going to clear out the old hall. That will be the venue for the competition, as it's got a stage and everything,' Mayor Bump said. 'And we'll put Ned's head back in its case there until we find a new home for it. I thought this would be a great way to say goodbye to the hall before we knock it all down. And let me add that Bump Construction will be sponsoring the competition, with the winner taking home a massive prize!'

He looked around the room. Still no excitement, just students staring.

'The prize will be free cement for a week to your parents, along with a tonne of bricks!'

Still nothing. Mayor Bump looked to his entourage, who just shrugged their shoulders back at him.

'I mean . . . the prize will be a family holiday to one of our new hotels in Spain, with a thousand euros spending money! How does that sound?'

Finally, the kids went mental, the teachers too. That prize sounded pretty amazing for a children's talent competition. Mayor Bump gave himself a round of applause, but his entourage looked a bit panicked. They had agreed to cement, not a holiday!

Onion was surprised, given that Mayor Bump was not known for being a generous man. He remembered what Grandad had said about him, that Bump wouldn't give you the steam off his pee.

AN ANNOUNCEMENT

Mrs Talcum was trying to restore order. Mr Brody, who was standing off to one side, shuffled forward and thanked Mayor Bump, though you could barely hear him over the commotion.

Onion crept forward through the crowd of kids, who were all milling around, waiting to get back to their classes and start making plans. He heard the new teacher offer his help to Mayor Bump, saying he'd like to assist in setting up the hall for the competition. Onion frowned. Here was a man he was sure was the Jackeen, who had broken into the hall last night and disguised himself as a teacher here today. Now he wanted to help with the work that was going on in the hall. Mr Brody was pushed aside as Mayor Bump was rushed out the door by his entourage as if he were the president and not just mayor of a small town no one had ever heard of.

Why was the Jackeen so interested in St Hilarius' National School?

Even so, Onion was tantalised by the thought of the talent competition. What kind of act could he put on? He wasn't great at singing and the only instrument he could play was the tin whistle, though the way he played it made it sound like a penguin trying to sing along with a trad band.

Onion's Top 5 Party Pieces

1. Turning his wonky eye in and out to the beat of any tune

2. Worrying so much that when he holds a light bulb it lights up slightly

3. The ability to rat on anyone in a mile radius when put under pressure

4. Winning staring competitions as his wonky eye is too distracting

5. Balancing his sister Molly on the ends of his feet as she sits on them

No, if he was going to be in with half a chance, he'd have to go with something else. As he followed his friends back to their classroom, they all chatted about their various skills and what they might bring to the stage.

By the end of the school day, Mr Brody had failed to teach the kids anything at all, apart from Clíona, who was just about able to make sense of some of the random guff he talked about. Now, however, the minds of the Five O's were on something else entirely. They headed back to Onion's, changed out of their school uniforms and got serious. They had work to do.

It was time to make a ghost.

CHAPTER TEN:
—
ROPES AND FAKE BLOOD

When Derek came home from school, he heard something going on down in the shed and went to take a look. Opening the door, he found the other Five O's staring at him in shock. They were in the process of tying ropes to the limbs of a mannequin, which they'd dressed in Grandad's old pyjamas . . . except they weren't his old ones. Grandad never bought anything for himself. Without realising it, they had taken Grandad's *only* pyjamas and splashed them with red spray-paint. Derek started to say something, frowned in bewilderment, then shook his head in disdain, snorted and closed the door again.

The Five O's all heaved a big sigh of relief. Moments later, the door opened again, and this time Molly was standing there.

'Whatcha doin'?' she asked.

'Nothing! Nothing!' Onion said, hurriedly stepping out and closing the door. 'It's just a thing for school. Where's Granny? Can you go and ask her if she'll let us have some bikkies? We're starving. We need a snack.'

'Yeah, okay,' Molly said.

She liked doing 'jobs' and this sounded like a chance to maybe get a biscuit for herself too, maybe even one from the fancy tin. She ran back up to the house, with hope in her heart.

'Good job that wasn't Granny,' Onion said as he came back in. 'She'd have a conniption if she saw us. We need to clear up here. Clíona, how are you doing with that balloon?

'Nearly ready,' she said, holding up a bulging red balloon. 'I think I might have overfilled it . . .'

As she lifted it, she fumbled and dropped it from her hands. It burst on the floor, spraying its contents everywhere, including their shoes and trousers.

'Aw, what?' Dallan groaned. 'Clíona! These are new shoes!'

'Sorry! I'm so sorry!'

The water was tinted red with food colouring, to try and make it look like blood. They'd tried to use red paint in the balloon, but it was too hard to pour in.

'Whatever,' Onion sighed, as he used a rag to wipe the worst of it off his legs and feet. 'Let's make another one and then we can go.'

Top 5 Worst Things to Spill on Your New Shoes

1. Clíona's Secret Stinkbomb Formula No. 8

2. Molly's sticky rainbow fairy dust – especially if you're a boy

3. Granny's sherry

4. Clíona's Secret Fake Poo Formula No. 4

5. Derek's favourite strawberry fruit drink
   – he'd see the stain, know you'd taken it,
   and give you dead arms all night long

Their ghostly mannequin was heavy and it was tricky getting it down to the woods behind the Valley. Onion held its shoulders, Clíona held the legs, and Dallan and Sive held each side of the body. They threw a blanket over it to hide it, but that just made it look even more suspicious.

'I defo got the heaviest end,' said Onion.

'It's just the bloomin' head. Me and Sive are carrying the body, which is the heaviest for sure,' moaned Dallan, out of breath.

'Excuse me, but the leg has the largest bone in the body and I'm carrying both of the femurs here, guys,' explained Clíona.

They might have attracted more attention if people weren't used to seeing the kids heading off to the piece of wasteland carrying a load of junk. Making camps down there was a time-honoured tradition. Or maybe people would think they were moving a dead body. They had to move fast, or at least as fast as you can move while carrying a mannequin.

As they approached the trees, they had to be more careful not to be spotted. They could hear the builders at work on the far side. They'd started levelling the ground and rebuilding the culvert, the tunnel the Big Leak flowed through under the road. That was a big job, and it would take them days.

The kids carried their big bundle into the shadow of the trees. As they passed the landmark known to the kids as 'the Hole', they each paused to perform a necessary ritual. The Hole was a set of stone slabs, hidden among the trees, with a small gap in the top. There was some kind of chamber or hollow inside, but nobody knew what it had been for. People often dropped stones into it, to listen to how long they took to fall. There were some very deep parts of the Hole, and it was considered lucky to get your stone to fall the furthest.

This is what the four kids did now, dropping in stones for luck. They'd need every bit they could get.

They knew where they needed to set up, in some bushes under the tall Scots pines close to the wasteland. Onion kept watch as they slung the ropes over some high branches and hauled the mannequin up into the foliage like a puppet, so that it was partially hidden from sight.

Onion felt a queasy sensation in his stomach when he saw a long, brand new, expensive-looking black Mercedes pull up on the far side of the bank of earth, near the entrance that had been created by the digger. Mayor Ronald Bump got out and the foreman came hurrying over to talk to him. Onion wondered if they should wait. He suspected Ronald Bump wasn't the type to be bothered by ghosts.

But it was all set up now. They were spread out, hiding under bushes near the bank of the stream. The mannequin was hanging high above them. Sive and Dallan were standing ready, holding the ropes, and Clíona had her phone ready, connected to a speaker, with clips of ghost sounds from a horror movie. They were pulling out all the stops here, taking it to the edge to save their beloved Valley.

The JCB was coming closer, but that was no good. The driver would never hear the ghost sounds over the growl of his engine. They needed some of the other workers to come closer, so they could get a proper scare when the ghost dropped down towards them. The four of them had to time it perfectly, for maximum effect. It had to come out of nowhere.

'Whatcha doin'?' a voice asked them.

It was Molly, standing there, a few metres in from the wasteland. Onion nearly screamed at her. What was she doing here? How did she get here? The driver of the JCB would see her at any second. She was going to ruin everything! Onion hissed at her and waved her over, and she was about to scamper over to him when a voice roared out at them.

'*Lift those legs! Tense that tum! Do it all together or you'll get a fat bum!*'

It gave Molly a fright and she let out a squeal. Onion gasped in shock. It was Clíona's FitChipper, which was on her *phone*, which was attached to a *speaker*. Everyone in the Valley had heard it, even over the engine of the digger.

'*Lift those legs! Tense that tum! Do it all together or you'll get a fat bum!*'

Onion dragged Molly out of sight and put a finger to his lips. The JCB driver was looking over his shoulder. He turned the digger around and drove close in to the trees.

'Now!' Sive said in a low voice. 'We have to do it *now*!'

CHAPTER ELEVEN:
THINGS GO TOO FAR

Sive and Dallan let go of their ropes and the headless mannequin dropped down out of the trees. But before it could swing down into sight, it got tangled on a branch. It was on Dallan's side, and he yanked hard on his ropes to free it. Clíona was fiddling with her phone, cutting off the FitChipper and trying to trigger the right sounds. Onion stared up at their ghost in dismay. It didn't look scary at all. It just looked like a goofy dummy in paint-stained rags dangling from some ropes.

It looked pathetic.

One rope broke off, falling loose into Dallan's hands. The mannequin swung down and slapped into the tree trunk over Sive's head. She frantically tried to haul it back up, but it spun out again.

Mayor Bump called out to the digger driver, who looked back, so he didn't see the dummy tumble out of the trees and land in the muddy stream with a loud splash. But the noise did draw some attention from the other builders, who were now on their way over. They'd heard a voice, and now a splash somewhere in the stream. Something was going on, but they couldn't see that part of the stream very well from where they were. They started forwards, with Ronald Bump not far behind. The digger driver peered into the shadows under the trees.

'Oi, is somebody in there?' he called out. 'Who's messing around?'

Onion pleaded with Molly to stay quiet and crawled over to Sive to help her with the ropes.

Together, they heaved as hard as they could, but the mannequin was stuck on something. Dallan scrambled over to help too. Molly was cowering under the bush where Onion had left her. *She* was the only one looking scared. It was all going wrong. Clíona finally got her phone working, and an eerie 'Oooooooooooohhh . . .' drifted through the woods.

Suddenly, the mannequin yanked free from whatever was holding it in the muck. The tension that the kids had been putting on the rope had bent the tree branch down, and now it sprang back up again, catapulting the mannequin out of the stream and up into the trees. The builders saw a strange shape fly up, just as Molly caught sight of it too. The ragged figure, plastered in mud now, adding a dirty mess to the red paint, flew in a high arc through the trees and soared out towards the digger.

The muddy, bloody, headless figure smacked against the windscreen of the JCB, the balloon

of red water on its chest bursting across the glass
as the ropes whipped across the sides of the cab,
spraying mud. Molly let out a shriek that burst
from the trees like a banshee's scream, causing
every bird to rise in an explosion of movement,
all of this combining to strike an animal terror
into the heart of the digger driver. He swung the
vehicle around, screaming, hit the accelerator
and tried to get away, but the headless body still
lay against his windscreen.

He swerved right and left, trying to shake the thing off. Mayor Bump and the other builders had to dive out of the way as the mighty vehicle and its panicked driver charged past them, heading for the road.

'Wait!' Mayor Bump yelled out. 'Hey, wait now! Hold on there!'

But it was too late. The driver was all over the place. He missed the big gap in the bank of earth that led out onto the road. Instead, the digger bellowed straight up the slope and plunged down the other side . . . right onto Mayor Bump's brand new Mercedes.

Onion would never forget the sound it made. Tonnes of construction machinery slamming down on a stylish new car worth tens of thousands of euros. Crumpling, tearing metal and shattering glass. One of these vehicles had been built for luxury and comfort, the other for years of heavy lifting work on building sites. The digger ended up sitting more-or-less upright, with just a few scratches. The thing that lay beneath it still looked slightly like a car, but a lot flatter, with bits sticking out at odd angles and loose pieces scattered on the ground around it.

Ronald Bump let out a wail and ran towards the remains of his car. The builders looked horrified, unsure of whether to follow their boss or investigate the trees, where the freaky figure had come from. Perhaps they were wondering which would be worse. After a few seconds' consideration, they went after their boss.

The Five O's stared at the scene, unable to move, unable to speak. Eventually, Sive managed a grunt. She tried again, still struggling to get a coherent word out. In the end, it was Dallan who was first to speak, after she'd poked him a few times.

'Yeah. Eh . . . yeah,' he croaked. 'We really need to go.'

They were close to crying as they ran, Sive and Dallan hauling Molly between them because they were the fastest runners. They were all in serious trouble. As he belted along, Onion tried to work out how much pocket money it would take to pay for a new Mercedes. Ten years' worth? Twenty? A hundred?

That car was probably worth as much as Granny and Grandad's house. Mayor Bump was definitely going to call the guards – not like the foreman who had threatened them with the *van especially designed for horrible children*. Bump would call for real. It wouldn't take the guards long to find out that the mannequin had come from the store in the old hall.

Onion gave a squeaky whimper and clutched his inhaler, which was bouncing all over his chest. What was he going to do? *What was he going to do*?

CHAPTER TWELVE:

A NEW THREAT

The Five O's ran out of steam just as they passed the school. They stopped there because they weren't sure where to go. Had anyone spotted them? Had they been recognised? Should they go home? Would the guards come looking for them? They sat on the wall of the school, catching their breaths and letting their nerves settle. Mr Oily Doyley was out cutting the grass of the playing field on his ride-on lawnmower.

Molly, at least, had calmed down and stopped screaming. She was in fine form now, hanging out with the bigger kids and getting to play their game with the big scary puppet, the digger and the funny squashed car. Onion had pleaded with her not to tell Granny, but he was *always* telling her not to tell Granny things and she hadn't decided if this was one of the serious ones or not yet.

They heard sirens then, and dropped down behind the wall, lifting their heads to peer over. A garda car sped past with The Ferg and Garda Judge staring intently ahead, no doubt responding to the emergency at the building site. Molly giggled, enjoying this new game.

Mr Oily Doyley saw them huddling behind the wall and steered his little tractor over towards them.

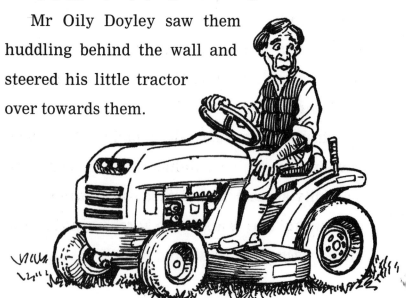

'Here, you kids, you're not supposed to be on school property after hours! Away with you now!'

As he came closer, he saw the expressions on their faces and realised they'd had some bad fright.

'Are yiz all right?' he asked. 'What's put the wind up you, now?'

Nobody wanted to answer. They just wanted him to go away. He was right, though – they weren't supposed to be on school property after school. But they didn't want to climb back over that wall either.

'Is that a new mower, Mr Oily, I mean Doyley . . . eh, Mr Doyle?' Clíona asked. 'It looks the business!'

'Thanks, love,' he said proudly. 'Yes, brand new! It's got a forty-two-inch cutting deck, with a six-fifty-six cc Briggs & Stratton V-twin engine and twin blades. This is the Lamborghini of the lawnmower world!'

'What are you going to do with the old one?' she asked.

'Ah, probably just scrap it. The engine's okay, but the chassis has rusted to pieces.'

Clíona asked a few more questions about the old mower and he was happy to answer. The other kids had no idea why she would be interested in a wreck of a lawnmower, but Mr Oily Doyley wasn't hassling them about being on school property anymore, so that was a good thing.

When Mr Oily Doyley got back to his mowing, he made no further attempt to move them on, so they were able to slump there against the wall and consider their futures.

Not much time had passed, and they were talking to each other in low voices, when a pretty, blonde-haired girl leaned over the wall and stared down at them.

'Well if it isn't the "Five Oh My God What Losers",' she said. 'What are you doing down there?'

A NEW THREAT

The Five O's tried to hide their fear. It was a bad idea to show fear around Tina Dalton. Two round, wide, dull-witted heads popped up either side of her at the wall, like huge, ugly moons orbiting the bright sun that was Tina's aura of power. These were the Bang-Off-Them Brothers, Barry and Larry Bang, Tina's enforcers, her robot slaves. Between the two of them, they had just enough intelligence to do what she told them, and that was never anything good.

Tina was the closest thing Ballinlud had to a Godmother of Crime. Adults loved her: she was smart, sophisticated, gorgeous, stylish and succeeded at most things school could throw at her. That angelic face, with its cream-coloured skin, big blue eyes and sharp nose, framed by blonde ringlets, looked like it could do no wrong. But adults rarely got to see her other side – the side other children saw. The Dark Side of Tina Dalton.

A lot of the kids paid their pocket money to Tina for protection, which meant protection from *Tina*. Because 'accidents' could happen. She ruled the schoolyard with an iron fist, ran the betting on all the kids' sports competitions and licensed the other bullies in the school. You actually had to pay for the right to be a bully in St Hilarius' National School. That was the price for operating on Tina's territory. Because 'accidents' could happen to bullies too.

'While I have you here,' she said, 'you should know that I'm going to win *Ballinlud's Got Talent*.

I'm going to be singing 'My Heart Will Go On', from that film *Titanic*. That holiday in Spain is mine. Is that understood?'

'What, are you going to cheat again, then?' Sive said, sniffing. 'Same old Tina.'

'It's not cheating,' Barry snarled. 'It's Winning by Any Means Necessary.'

'Yeah,' Larry added. 'Tina *has* to win. It's her mani– . . . her mafi– . . . her . . . eh . . .'

'*Manifest destiny*,' Tina prompted, rolling her eyes.

Sive also rolled her eyes at that, showing that she was even better at eye rolling than Tina, and that she could chew gum at the same time.

'What does that mean?' Onion asked.

'It means her domination is both justified and inevitable,' Dallan told him.

'And *it is*,' Tina said firmly.

'Yeah,' said Barry.

'Yeah,' said Larry.

Top 5 Competitions Tina Has Won by Cheating

1. The Ballinlud Dog Show – she used someone else's dog

2. The St Hilarius' National School Handwriting Contest – everybody else's pens mysteriously leaked

3. Pin the Tail on the Donkey at Emma Smith's birthday party – she stuck the pin in Emma Smith!

4. The Ballinlud Junior Beauty Contest – the only other girl who could compete with her got a big wad of chewing gum stuck in her hair and had to shave her head

5. The Inter-Schools Basketball League Final – someone put sneezing powder in the opposing team's towels

'We're not scared of you, you know,' Dallan said.

'Eh, I am,' said Onion with confidence.

'Of course you are,' she chuckled. 'You're nothing but tongue fungus, the lot o' yiz. And I'm the toothbrush. Show up if you want, make it look convincing, but just so we're clear, you're going to lose, got it?'

'The whole school will want to take part in this,' Sive pointed out. 'How are you going to make sure *everyone* else does a worse act than you?'

'That's for me to know and you to find out,' Tina said, tapping the side of her nose.

'Yeah,' said Barry.

'Yeah,' said Larry.

'And if I think you're going to show me up,' she added. 'Well . . . accidents happen, don't they?'

CHAPTER THIRTEEN:
—
KEEPING SECRETS

When Onion finally worked up the nerve to go home, mainly because both his and Molly's stomachs were demanding their dinner, he half expected the guards to be waiting for him. The other Five O's had split off to head back to their own houses. Onion now trudged down the side of the house to the back door, leading Molly by the hand, bracing himself for whatever was coming.

'Where the hell were you two?' Granny screamed.

Uh-oh, here we go, thought Onion.

'I noticed Molly was missing and I was so worried. I even sent Grandad off to Olive Branch's house, the mad lady with the cats, because Molly loves to go to there. He's furious – she made him sit with her and talk about cats for ages.'

'Sorry, Granny. The school's having a talent show on Saturday so we were just . . . rehearsing. Molly really wanted to help. You know how much she loves jobs,' said Onion, trying to keep his wonky eye in check.

'The school's having a talent show on Saturday?!' Granny exclaimed, launching into chatty mode. 'Onion, this is only brilliant! What are you going to do for your act?'

Onion was taken aback. It took a few seconds to change mental gear and pull his mind away from the catastrophe he'd left behind in the Valley.

'I . . . eh . . . I . . . uh, I think I'd like to do some stand-up comedy,' he said.

'That's the funniest thing you've ever said,' Derek snorted. He was sitting at the table, having a cup of tea and staring at his phone. 'You should lead with that one.'

'Get lost!' Onion snapped at him. He wasn't in the mood for Derek's hassle.

'Mind your language, pet!' Granny said. 'Now, comedy, eh? That's a tough gig. I "walked the boards" a little when I was young, you know, so I can give you some tips on stage performance. You'll need a good costume too!'

Onion threw a look of alarm at Derek, who put a hand over his mouth to hide a smile. There was no telling what ideas Granny had about what a comedian should wear, but Onion wanted people laughing at his jokes, not his dress sense.

'I think just my usual T-shirt and jeans, Granny,' he said. 'It's what everybody wears now.'

'Nonsense! We'll have to get you kitted out in something *special*,' she insisted. 'Leave it with me.'

'There you are, Molly,' said Grandad. 'I'll kill ye, Onion. You should have said you'd taken her out with you. Now as punishment you can get me my basin and Dettol so I can soak my feet. Your brain is connected to your feet and right now my brain is pumping with the noise of that looper cat woman. I'll be in the living room.'

Onion prepared the basin of water with Dettol, one of Grandad's favourite evening-time rituals, and delivered it to the living room.

It was six o'clock and the news was on. Grandad was listening to the telly as he read the newspaper, a double dose of what was going on in the world.

There was a reporter talking about the Jackeen. Onion sat down on the sofa to watch. It didn't make him feel any better. The Jackeen, real name unknown, was thought to be responsible for a string of high-profile burglaries and heists in Ireland and the UK. He was considered

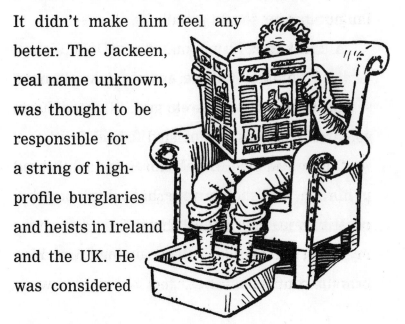

extremely intelligent, ruthless and there were very few photos of him because he was also a master of disguise.

'I *knew* it!' Onion said quietly. 'It *is* him!'

'It is who?' Derek said, coming into the room. 'What are you on about?'

'Nothing,' Onion retorted. 'Unless you want to get back with the Five O's again and help us out. It's a secret.'

'It can stay a secret then. I couldn't care less, ye dope, ye,' Derek grunted. 'I keep telling you, I'm not in your stupid gang!'

'All right, then. I'll tell you anyway,' Onion sighed.

'He's going to tell me anyway, just after me saying I don't care,' Derek said. 'Right, off you go. I won't get this part of my life back.'

Onion motioned Derek closer and whispered in his ear. 'Don't tell anyone, but I think our new substitute teacher is the Jackeen.'

Derek burst out laughing, causing Grandad to look up from his paper.

'What are you two messing about at?' he said. 'Can a man not catch up on a bit of news in his own house without you two distracting him? Get on out of here if you're not going to be quiet.'

'Grandad, Onion thinks his new teacher is the Jackeen,' Derek told him.

'Derek!' Onion protested.

'What are you on about, Onion?' Grandad asked, lowering his paper to frown at his grandson. 'What would he be doing in your school? Why would *anyone* go to school if they didn't have to? He'd have to be off his head.'

Onion blinked. *He'd have to be off his head.* Onion had been trying to figure out why the master thief would be hanging around his school. Why would St Hilarius' National School be of interest to a guy who stole art and jewels and robbed *banks*? But it had been right there in front of Onion the whole time. How had he not thought about it before? The head of Ned Belly.

'The Jackeen is trying to find Ned Belly's treasure,' Onion said.

'You're an idiot,' Derek replied.

.

CHAPTER FOURTEEN:

SCARY STORIES

O n Thursday morning, everyone at school was talking about the accident at the building site. None of the kids, apart from the Five O's, of course, knew exactly what had happened. There was a rumour that there was a ghost down in the Valley. Some offered the opinion that it was Ned Belly's ghost, and to use Youssef's words: 'Disaster has been visited upon those who have disturbed Ned Belly's rest.'

Youssef was the go-to guy for knowledge of all matters concerning the supernatural, thanks to all the horror stories he'd watched and read. It was only natural that he'd gain a big audience after this new event. When Onion arrived in, there was a large group of kids already in the yard, sitting on the ground around Youssef's wheelchair, listening to him give his opinions on the terrors to be found in the Valley and the area surrounding the Big Leak.

Top 5 Scariest Things to Happen in Ballinlud

1. The day the JCB was possessed by the ghost of Ned Belly and crushed Mayor Ronald Bump's car

2. The day a tree fell down and the branches made the shape of Jesus – people arrived in their droves to pray at the tree

3. The day the Big Leak became an even bigger leak

4. The day the rumour went around that head lice could burrow into your brain

5. The day the priest went missing for a week – it turned out he had just changed into casual clothes and no one noticed him

As Youssef was talking, Onion saw Clíona walk up and ask him something. He didn't hear the question or the reply, but then she took out a measuring tape and started measuring Youssef's wheelchair. When he noticed that the crowd was dispersing, he decided to ask a question of his own.

'Hey, Youssef, does anyone know where Ned Belly's house actually was? Like, it was supposed to be by the Big Leak, right? But where?'

'Nobody knows for sure, Onion,' Youssef replied, shaking his head thoughtfully. 'Word on the forums is that Cromwell had it destroyed after they chopped off Ned's head. And then farmers ended up using all the stones for walls and such, so after a few years, there was nothing left at all. Why do you ask? You thinking of looking for the treasure?'

'Well no, but . . .'

'Because you've heard the warnings, mate.'

'Yeah, sure.'

'It wouldn't end well, that's all I'm saying.'

'No, I've got that. But . . .'

'Although, if you really *did* want to search for it,' Youssef continued, 'I'd be up for that.'

'Really?'

'Sure. How often do you get to investigate a legendary curse and search for hidden treasure in your own back yard, right? It'd be cool, man. I'm right up for that!'

Onion nodded. He was quite taken with the idea of searching for treasure, but he was more interested in why the Jackeen was here.

He and Youssef agreed to meet at break time to talk it out some more, and then they headed for class.

Mr Brody, too, appeared to be intrigued by what happened in the Valley yesterday. Once everyone had sat down, he asked if anyone had seen the incident. He seemed to look extra hard at Onion, whose wonky eye was doing everything it could to scream for attention, like someone trapped in a house and hammering on the window in the hope of being seen by passers-by. Mr Brody turned awkwardly to the whiteboard and began to write on it. As he did, the barping started again. He sounded like a bouncy castle when everyone tried to get off at the same time.

'Does anyone . . .'

BAAAAAAAAARRRRRRRRP . . .

'. . . know the rhyme . . .'

BAAAAAAAAARRRRRRRRP . . .

'. . . associated with . . .'

BAAAAAAAAARRRRRRRRP . . .

'. . . the legend of Ned Belly?'

Everyone in the class suddenly became very interested in their desks, afraid to look up in case Mr Brody asked them to recite the rhyme.

'You with the eye patch, off you go,' said Mr Brody as he walked towards Onion, his protruding bum getting stuck between a few desks along the way.

Onion was so terrified he couldn't remember the rhyme. 'When Ned was dead, they took his head. Ehh . . . umm ... And then they hid it in a . . . shed?'

Mr Brody glared into Onion's face with his beady eyes. Onion thought he was a goner for sure, but thankfully Youssef saved the day.

'I know the rhyme, sir,' said Youssef.

'Proceed,' said Brody, spinning to face Youssef with a quick and loud BARP!

'When Ned was dead, they took his head,
But no one listened when he said,
I'll die before you take my gold,
So keep back now 'cos you've been told,
The rise of spring in Ballinlud,
Will hide the place beneath its flood,
I curse you all who'd steal what's mine,
You'll search and search and see no sign,
The secret's lost with sly old Ned,
Hidden there in his dead head.'

Onion lifted his head. There were two lines he hadn't heard before.

'The rise of spring in Ballinlud
Will hide the place beneath its flood.'

Onion was sure Granny hadn't included those in the version she'd recited, and he wasn't sure what they meant. Mr Brody seemed to think there should be more too, because he asked the other kids if they knew any other lines to the rhyme.

Perhaps, like all the Irish legends, there were different versions of the poem. Not that it mattered. There was nothing in the rhyme that could tell you where the treasure was, only a warning not to search for it. And if Youssef wasn't scared of seeking it out, despite all his knowledge of curses and violent deaths, then Onion wasn't going to be scared either.

He was sure the other Five O's would want to get involved too. Well, maybe not Derek, but the others would. As Youssef had said, who *wouldn't* want to look for hidden treasure?

CHAPTER FIFTEEN:
—
HIGH EXPECTATIONS

Mr Brody decided that they would all help him start preparing the old hall for the talent show. He seemed eager to get inside the old hall, and the kids were happy to escape the classroom and Brody's lectures about quantum physics for a while, so off they went.

Once they started work on the hall, however, it quickly became clear that Mr Brody had no awareness of health and safety. He wanted all the big things moved outside into the yard. The furniture and other junk, some of it very heavy, was stacked in unstable piles that teetered when the children started to take things from them.

THE HEAD OF NED BELLY

There were broken panes of glass and mirrors, and various pieces of spiky metal that were either medieval weapons or some form of wrought-iron decorations from back in the days when schools had dungeons.

The place was so dusty that Onion could feel his asthma tugging at his lungs. The air filled with it as they started moving things around. The kids were getting distracted too, playing tag among the little rabbit runs between the stacks, knocking into things and generally messing about.

Clíona kept finding curious objects to look at and examine. Dallan wouldn't stop talking, as he often did when he was excited, whether or not anyone was listening. Sive was protesting that she knew her rights and children could not be used for manual labour like this. Onion was hanging around Mr Brody, trying to see through his disguise.

At one point, Dallan and Mr Brody were trying to haul the glass display case outside when the teacher tripped against Onion's feet. His protruding bottom hit Onion's belly, there was another BARP! and his hand slipped, so the bulky piece of furniture dropped on his foot. Mr Brody let out a furious yelp and a string of curse words that a normal teacher would *never* use in front of their pupils. He yanked his foot out from under the case and stumbled backwards into Onion, hitting him harder this time.

Onion thought that Mr Brody's body felt weird, as if it was a lot lighter than it looked. Almost as if there wasn't really a *body* there at all. Something about the size and shape of a large wallet dropped out of the back of his jacket

and landed on the floor, bouncing under a table. Dallan saw it fall and caught Onion's eye.

For once, Dallan didn't say anything, but his look said it all: don't even think about it.

Onion winced, shrugging helplessly. He couldn't just ignore it, could he? The kids were making so much noise that Mr Brody didn't hear the wallet fall. He turned around and scowled at Onion.

'Can't you make yourself useful, instead of loitering about and getting in my way?'

The display case was the one that had once held Ned Belly's head. Onion moved over beside Dallan and helped Mr Brody carry it outside. It was really heavy. Onion and Dallan kept having to put their side down, much to Brody's annoyance. The teacher was clearly much stronger than both of them together and could lift his side with ease.

'Mr Brody!'

They all turned to see who was speaking. It was Mrs Talcum, who was standing there with shock on her face.

'That hall is not a safe environment for the children,' she said firmly. 'And they should not be hauling around heavy bits of furniture and handling scrap pieces of metal and broken glass.'

'That's what *I* told him!' Sive called from inside.

'You *know* we have some men coming to clear the place and make it fit for purpose,' Mrs Talcum said. 'Why do you have the children doing it?'

'I thought it might be a good experience for them,' Brody replied, appearing unruffled by Mrs Talcum's objections. 'There's so much of interest in here. It seems a shame not to make the most of it.'

Onion used the distraction to slip back inside. Crawling under the table, he spotted the black leather wallet that had fallen from Mr Brody's jacket. Thinking it might hold some ID, Onion picked it up, hoping to prove that his teacher was not who he claimed to be.

It had a zip around the edge to keep it closed and, being careful to keep in out of sight, Onion opened it up. His hands were shaking as he did so. He'd be in serious trouble if he was caught interfering with this.

He was so *sure* he'd finally find some evidence . . . and yet there were no cards or documents or even money in the wallet. Instead, he found a selection of what looked like dentist's tools: thin steel handles with spines sticking out of them, formed into different kinds of hooks or curves or grooves. Then Dallan appeared, crawling in beside him.

'Okay, what've we got then?

Onion gazed at the tools in confusion, trying to work out what he was looking at.

'I don't get it. Mr Brody's a . . . a *dentist*?'

CHAPTER SIXTEEN:
TOOLS OF THE TRADE

Onion had *intended* to give Mr Brody's wallet of tools back to him, but he dithered about it for an hour or so. By the time he'd decided to do it, Dallan and Sive told him he'd held onto it for too long and it would now look suspicious. How would he explain what he'd been doing with it all this time? Onion wished he could figure out what the tools were. Of all the Five O's, Clíona was the most likely to know what these things were for, but she'd disappeared at lunchtime, before Onion had a chance to talk to her alone, and didn't come back to class.

Clíona did this sometimes. She had been badly bullied for a couple of years in school until she'd met Onion and the others, who were always there to back her up now. Her mother, Vlasta O'Hare, had always told her that she could come home at any time if she wanted to, as long as she told her teachers. Her house was only a ten-minute walk up the road. The teachers had complained to Vlasta about this on a number of occasions, but Clíona's mother was a formidable woman.

'When you can promise me she'll never be bullied again . . . *ever*,' she told them once, 'I'll promise you she'll stay in school.'

There wasn't much the teachers could say to that, particularly as Clíona kept up with her school work, easily achieved the grades she needed, and read more challenging books than most of the teachers. Now, just when the Five O's needed her technical brain, she had disappeared again.

TOOLS OF THE TRADE

After lunch, it was obvious Mr Brody was bothered about something. His class wasn't quite as ridiculous as before. He let the pupils look at their textbooks for some of the time, which they did with a great sense of relief. The teacher's unease might have been down to the fact that he had dropped something and couldn't find it, though it was interesting that he hadn't asked anyone about it. Onion wondered why.

Perhaps he didn't want anyone to know about the dentist's tools.

All through the school, children were either talking about *Ballinlud's Got Talent* and rehearsing their acts, or trying to find out what other acts they were up against. Tina Dalton had put out the word around the school: if anyone else was considering doing the song from *Titanic* – or even a similar power ballad with an uplifting key change – they'd better have their airplane ticket bought and a taxi booked for the airport.

One poor girl made the mistake of singing a few bars of Ariana Grande's 'One Last Time' during lunch and the Bang-Off-Them Brothers heard her. She ran home crying with yoghurt poured over her head and soup in her schoolbag.

It was an hour to going-home time when the van for a security company pulled into the car park. They had a fancy new display case for Ned Belly's head, with a steel frame and reinforced glass, all designed to be wired into the school's alarm system. It was installed in a small room at the near end of the old hall, where they also set up security cameras and motion sensors. The children watched with interest through the window as the man and woman went back and forth with their pieces of equipment.

Mr Brody watched too.

The head itself was being kept in a safety-deposit box in the bank until it was time for it to move back. Mayor Bump had decided the leathery, mummified head would inspire the children to reach for the same heights of fame that Ned himself had achieved.

Perhaps one day, Dallan had commented, Tina Dalton's head would be preserved for all time in a glass box too. This got a laugh, but then everybody winced. If that ever got back to Tina, Dallan might find his own head being put out on display.

And so, by the time the bell rang to end the school day, the display stand was ready to receive the head of Ned Belly back in its place of honour in the old hall. It would be placed there on the day of the competition, and would stay there until the building was ready to be demolished.

After two dramatic evenings, the Five O's decided they'd all stay in their own homes that evening, to relax and watch some telly. Besides, there was still a lot of heat around the destruction of Mayor Ronald Bump's car, so they figured they should keep a low profile for while.

Once he'd done his homework, Onion went up to his room to look at the wallet of steel implements, to try and work out why a master thief would have dentist's tools. There was no internet in the house, apart from on Derek's phone, and Derek spent most of his pocket money paying for credit. Asking to use his phone was like asking to borrow the eyes from his sockets.

Onion was staring at the thin pieces of steel, hoping against hope that the answer would come out of nowhere, when something did actually smack across his head, making him drop the open wallet.

TOOLS OF THE TRADE

It was Derek, holding a copy of *SCORE!*, the football magazine, which he'd just swung at Onion's head. It wasn't a hard hit, but it was annoying, as only a big brother could make it. Onion scowled at him and waved him away. He bent down to pick up the wallet, only to have Derek beat him to it.

'Hey, gimme that!' Onion shouted.

He went to grab for it and then stopped when he saw the expression on Derek's face. His brother held up the tools, frowning in what almost looked like concern.

'Where did you get these?'

'Why? Do you know what they are?'

'Whose are these, Onion? They're not yours. You could be in serious trouble for having these.'

'Mr Brody dropped it, and I . . . I picked it up. I thought they were dentist's tools . . .'

'Dentist's tools? You're sure *Brody* dropped this wallet?'

'. . . Yes, but I couldn't figure out why he . . . why the Jackeen would have them. Maybe they're for interrogating people? Like, he could poke at . . . at someone's fillings or . . . or stick one of those things up their nose, like, you know? But he *is* the Jackeen, Derek, I'm telling you! And don't say–'

'I believe you,' Derek said.

'I . . . you what?' Onion stuttered into silence, thinking he couldn't have heard that right.

'I believe you,' his brother said again. 'Or at least, *something's* up with that teacher of yours. Onion, these aren't dentist's tools, they're *lockpicks*. This is a really professional set of lockpicks. You know, the things *thieves* use for opening locks when they don't have a key?'

'How are you so sure?' Onion asked.

'Matt Malcolm's bigger brother, Dennis Malcom, is five years older than him and has a full moustache. He's seen it all. I mean, a full moustache! I remember him showing me a set of these in his house,' answered Derek.

'Oh my God, is Matt Malcolm's older brother Dennis Malcolm with the moustache a thief?'

shrieked Onion. 'Maybe he's an accomplice to the Jackeen . . .'

WHACK!

'Owwwwwwwwwwwwww!' Onion rubbed his head as Derek put his *SCORE!* magazine down again.

'No, ye tool,' said Derek. 'His dad is a locksmith. But what matters is, you could be right, though I flippin' hate to admit it. Mr Brody might be the Jackeen. Maybe we should call the guards.'

'We can't call the guards!' Onion said in fright.

'Why not?'

Onion told him about the prank in the Valley that had gone so badly wrong, about the puppet and Molly's scream and the runaway JCB and the squashed car and how the guards were investigating it all. Derek listened with growing amazement and then creased up laughing.

'Oh, Onion . . . man. That was *you lot*? You crack me up! Hahaha! You cabbages! There's no bad situation you can't make worse, is there, bro?

All right then, no guards. It looks like we'll have to handle this on our own.'

And though he didn't say it out loud, Onion felt a huge wave of relief to have his big brother on his side. All five of the Five O's, together again. Maybe things were going to work out after all.

'This is just a one-time deal, though,' Derek told him. 'I'm still not in your stupid gang.'

CHAPTER SEVENTEEN:
BRODY'S PLACE

Derek was curious now, and he thought in ways that Onion didn't. Onion told him his theory, that the Jackeen was searching for Ned Belly's gold. Derek didn't buy that. The Jackeen was a hardened criminal. He wouldn't be here for some fairy story about a miser's gold. Derek said he wanted to learn more about Mr Brody. The first thing was to find out what he got up to after school.

'We need to find out where he lives,' he said.

'Really?' Onion said nervously. 'Are you sure? You mean, following a teacher home? That sounds a bit, you know, *creepy*? I don't want to . . .'

'You were the one who said no guards, Onion,' Derek said firmly. 'So we have to do our own investigating. Now are we doing this or what?'

'Yeah, I suppose,' Onion murmured. 'But Mr Brody drives home. I . . . I noticed that. Not that I was spying on him or anything . . . So, how are we going to find out where he lives?'

'I know some people,' Derek told him. 'Let me reach out to a few of my contacts and let's see what they can dig up.'

'Matt Malcolm's brother Dennis Malcolm with the moustache?' asked Onion.

'The very man,' said Derek, as he looked out the window to the garden like he was talking about some guru high in the hills of Tibet.

It turned out that Derek's 'contact' was able to dig up Mr Brody's address.

The address had them both wondering, though. It was in a business park on the road between Ballinlud and Dundeer, one of those places with big building units, grey boxes that could be made into a tile centre or a garden centre or a play centre, just by moving the interior walls around. Nobody lived in a place like that.

Except it seemed that Mr Brody did.

Onion and Derek got their bikes out and cycled to Flowery Meadows Business Park, four estates over. It was a bland, concrete-and-tarmac place with a grid of roads lined with dry grass and dead bushes. And, of course, row after row of buildings that all looked the same, apart from the logos on the front.

It was after hours, and most of the businesses were closed at six, so the estate was quiet. Somewhere, they could hear the buzz of what sounded like a motorbike, zipping around on the roads. This wasn't unusual. It was the kind of place where learner drivers came to practise their manoeuvres and boy racers came to scream around in cars or on motorbikes. This didn't sound like a very big bike, buzzing like a mosquito the way it did, but it did mean that Onion and Derek might be spotted, and they were careful to keep track of the sound.

The address brought them to a big office space above a plumbing centre on the corner of one of the anonymous sites. The door was around the side, with a small sign next to it that read BUBBLE WRAP FACTORY. Onion knew that Mr Brody drove a Ford Focus. It wasn't parked anywhere nearby, so hopefully he wasn't around. At first, the boys didn't know what to do. Then Onion spotted a fire escape around the back, the stairs partly hidden by some wheelie bins and a skip full of bubble-wrap leftovers.

They were about to start up the metal stairs when they heard the motorbike approaching. The boys dived into the skip. As they landed among the bubble wrap, it sounded like popcorn being made. Thank God Molly wasn't there. She'd have screamed at each pop.

POP . . .   POP . . .POP . . . .

POP . . . POP

'Stop moving about,' hissed Derek.

POP . . .

POP . . .   POP . . . .

POP . . .   POP

'I'm trying my best,' whispered Onion.

POP . . .

POP . . . POP . . . .

POP . . .

POP

'Oh for God's sake, just lie still,' moaned Derek.

POP . . . . . . PIPPP

The air finally left the last bit of bubble wrap as Onion and Derek laid still.

They listened to the buzzing pass by, growing louder and then quieter again. There was a faint sound of tyres squealing, and then the engine noises started off down another road.

The two brothers were howling laughing as they tried to get out of the skip. They kept falling back into the bubble wrap as they tried to help each other out.

POP . . .

POP . . . POP . . .

PIPPP . . .

POP . . .   POP

They may have tried to kill each other at home, but out here they were members of the Five O's and that bond was sacred.

Well, at least Onion thought so. Derek was just laughing at the noise and watching Onion fall a lot, sucking on his inhaler and trying to fix his eyepatch and glasses.

Finally, they were out. They began to climb the stairs.

There was a line of windows at the first-floor level, and a short walkway below them, so once they'd reached the top of the steps, they could see into different parts of the office within. The Venetian blinds were down, though they were all buckled and bent, the way blinds got when they were yanked up and down too much, so it was still possible to see inside.

The light was dim. There were only these windows, and another few around the corner, also covered with blinds, but the boys could see that it was a bare, square space stretching into the gloom. It was about the size of a large garage, with a couple of doors at the far end.

There was almost nothing in the room. From where he was standing, with his hands cupped around his face to block the shine from the glass, Onion could see a tall, grey metal cabinet with a secure lock on it, a couple of suitcases and a camp bed neatly made up. He moved to another window and spotted a table, the kind with foldable legs. There was a laptop sitting on it, facing an ordinary office swivel chair. Most of the space was left empty, and there were lines marked on the floor with masking tape. Onion thought they might represent the positions of walls or furniture. It was like the plan of a room, marked out for practising something.

'It's like he hardly lives here at all,' Derek muttered. 'This isn't a home, it's a safe house or . . . or a base of operations. He's planning a *heist*, Onion. But what's he going to steal?'

'I told you,' Onion replied. 'He's here for Ned Belly's gold!'

'Don't be daft. This is serious business. This guy's not here to mess around.'

They moved along again, and Onion came to the window nearest the corner. Putting his hands up to the sides of his face, he peered in to see if he could spot anything else.

As he did, he heard the buzzing of the motorbike coming back.

Onion and Derek were completely exposed up there on the walkway. Anyone coming around the corner, down the road to the side of the building, could see them out the back. They had to get out of sight.

Onion risked one last look before he had to move. Peeking through the slats in the blinds, he scanned the room. He had to pull his head around to a funny angle because his eyepatch blocked off his left eye. The buzzing of the engine was getting louder. But suddenly Onion noticed, standing there, *right there beside the window*, just off to one side of him, was a tall, stocky figure in a black suit and tie and a white shirt. A cold shudder went down Onion's spine. No, it wasn't just some guy standing there in the darkness. And it wasn't Mr Brody.

Because this figure *had no head*.

Stricken with panic, Onion stumbled back away from the window, felt something block his way behind him and, without thinking, he scrambled over it. The thing blocking his way was the safety rail. There wasn't anything on the other side of it but thin air.

Too late to save himself, Onion knew he'd just tumbled backwards off the walkway, and now he was plunging towards the tarmac below.

CHAPTER EIGHTEEN:

YOUSSEF'S NEW WHEELS

POP!

The landing was louder but not quite as hard as he'd expected. Yes, it hurt, and his brain felt like it had fallen out the bottom of his head, but he'd expected more crunching of flesh and bone and not so much . . . popping. The skip. He'd landed in the skip.

'What did you jump for?' Derek asked in a grating growl, hopping down the steps towards him. 'You're mental, you are.'

Onion was groaning in pain. While sheets of unwanted bubble wrap were far better for landing on than tarmac, it still hurt a lot.

And he'd lost his glasses too. None of this, however, served to erase that last moment on the walkway and what he'd seen.

'Brody's got no head,' he wheezed. 'He's up there and he's got no head. Or . . . or it's somebody. There's . . . there's somebody up there and he's got no head.'

By this time, the motorbike had grumbled to a halt and they heard hushed voices.

'Okay, you can come out of there,' a familiar voice called. 'We saw you. And even if we didn't, we could hear you from Ballinlud. It's like a fireworks display in there. Onion, come on, we know it's you.'

Onion whimpered, fumbled around until he found his glasses and, with great difficulty, he raised his head above the rim of the skip. For a minute, he thought he'd hit his head harder than he had and was now concussed . . . or in shock, or whatever it was that made you see things that weren't there. He found himself looking at Clíona and Youssef, who was sitting in a thing that looked like a cross between a wheelchair and a motocross bike.

The machine's engine was chugging quietly. Youssef was wearing swimming goggles, presumably to protect his eyes from the wind as he reached speeds beyond those of a conventional wheelchair.

'What . . . what is that?' Onion said, his words slurred.

'Why are you spying on us?' Clíona asked, ignoring his question. She was standing on a step on the back of the weird machine. 'We came here so Youssef could try this out without anyone bothering him. Can't you give us some privacy?'

'But *what is it*?' Derek repeated the question.

'I made it for him. He needed a wheelchair with a motor, but his family couldn't afford one, so I made him one,' Clíona replied, shrugging, as if this was a completely normal thing to do. 'It's . . . made of a few things. A bit of wheelchair, obviously, and some motorbike wheels for the back and go-kart wheels for the front. And a game's joystick. And the engine from Mr Oily Doyley's old lawnmower.'

'They'll never let you take that into school,' Derek said. 'That's like . . . it's a *vehicle*, Youssef. And besides, it's giving off smoke. You can't smoke in school. You can't drive that into a classroom.'

'You wanna bet?' Youssef said defiantly.

'Anyway!' Clíona snapped. 'We came here to test it out. Why did you have to follow us?'

'We didn't come here to spy on you,' Onion babbled blearily. 'We were trying to see where Mr Brody lived. Derek found the address. Well, Matt Malcolm's brother Dennis Malcolm with the moustache found it. But that's beside the point . . . and . . . and we were able to get up on the fire escape and look in the windows and . . . and . . . and see that there's almost nothing up there, although it looks like he's planning a big heist only . . . only . . . somebody's up there staring out at us and . . . and . . . THEY HAVE NO HEAD!'

Onion's eye was flying in and out a lot, looking at his nose and back out again. The wonky eye was in full-on panic!

There was a few seconds of silence while this all sank in, and then Derek and Clíona jumped from their respective positions and raced up the stairs.

'Hey, that's not fair!' Youssef yelled after them. 'Spooky stuff is *my* area of expertise and *I don't do stairs!*'

Top 5 Things Youssef Hates

1. Stairs

2. Badly plotted horror films

3. Doors that open towards you

4. Top shelves

5. Tina Dalton

It occurred to Onion that if the headless man was going to burst out of the office after them, it would have happened by now. With painful, awkward movements, he hauled himself out of the skip – again – and tramped up the stairs. The other two were staring in through the window he'd fled from only minutes before.

'I don't believe it,' Derek said, squinting through the glass. 'It's a blow-up bodysuit!'

'What do you mean?' Onion asked, trying to see past them.

'There are these suits you can blow up and they make you look bigger, completely different from your ordinary body,' his brother replied. 'Or ones that can make you look fat. It's hanging from a stand, still in its clothes, which is why you thought it was standing up. This one's got loads of padding, so Brody must look twice his normal width. It's part of his disguise, I suppose. If you're looking for a . . . a sinewy cat burglar, you're not going to look twice at a guy who's the shape of a Portaloo and sounds like a bouncy castle when he walks.' He turned to Clíona. 'Onion found a wallet Brody dropped too. It was a set of lock-picks.'

Clíona took another look at the blow-up bodysuit and then looked back at her friends.

'You were right, Onion,' she said, in her straightforward way. 'Brody is the Jackeen. I'm sorry I didn't believe you.'

'No one ever believes me,' said Onion.

'Well, this time I know it's the truth, Onion,' answered Clíona.

'How?' asked Onion.

'That eye of yours, pal. It's on overdrive. You're either totally lying or telling the truth, and right now you're telling the truth!' smiled Clíona.

There came a roar of an engine from down below and Youssef shouted up at them.

'Oi! What's up there? Will one of you batterballs please tell me *what the flip is going on*?!'

CHAPTER NINETEEN:

AN APPEAL FOR INFORMATION

I t was Friday morning. Another assembly was called at St Hilarius' National School, and this time the stage had been pulled out. There was an upright human-sized shape covered in a white sheet standing on the stage when the children came in and, for a minute, Onion thought they were going to be learning about ghosts. When he mentioned this to Sive, she rolled her eyes at him, and put some gum in her mouth. They weren't supposed to chew gum in school, but this was her thing and she figured there was safety in a crowd.

The pupils all filed into their usual lines. As the teachers got them settled, Mrs Talcum came into the hall with two guards. It was The Ferg and Garda Judge. The Ferg was looking inflated with importance, while his partner contented herself with glaring at the children from behind her sunglasses. Her expression implied that they were all guilty of something and she knew exactly what.

'Good morning, children,' Mrs Talcum said in a tired voice. 'We won't keep you for long, but Gardas Plunkett and Judge would like our help in a matter, and I want you all to give them your full attention. Garda Plunkett?'

'Thank you, Mrs Talcum,' The Ferg said, his hat in his hands as he put on the stern but tolerant look he'd seen on the guards who got to make these announcements on TV. It was his biggest wish to be the one who made announcements on TV. 'Now then, boys and girls, we . . . that is, *An Garda Síochána* . . . are launching an appeal for information regarding the events in the vicinity of the top of the Diddle River on Wednesday last at four twenty-five or thereabouts.'

THE HEAD OF NED BELLY

The pupils of St Hilarius' took a few seconds to struggle with this sentence. A lot of the younger kids couldn't make any sense of it at all.

'You mean that thing where Ned Belly's ghost attacked the builders at the Big Leak and possessed the JCB and squashed Mayor Bump's car?' Youssef called out. 'Is it *those* events you're talking about?'

Youssef was back in his normal wheelchair now. His new one was still in the testing phase. Hearing the situation laid out like that in front of everyone, Onion put his face in his hands. Dallan gulped. Sive didn't roll her eyes. Clíona started whistling loudly, trying to act casual, until Sive elbowed her in the ribs to make her stop. A few of the pupils who were slower on the uptake made 'Oh' expressions, and were now nodding in understanding. This was the first time most of them had heard that the Big Leak was actually the top end of the river known as the Diddle. The Ferg, however, was not happy at being interrupted.

An Appeal for Information

'That is not the accepted interpret . . . interpreta . . . reading of the facts of this case,' he said to Youssef, trying to hide his annoyance at not being able to say 'interpretation'. 'It is believed that the builders were the victims of a malicious prank. It is alleged that the pranksters set up an elaborate hoax using this mannequin, exhibit A . . .' He gave Youssef a hard stare as he whipped the sheet off the dummy on the stage: '. . . to *simulate* the *appearance* of a ghost.'

There was a gasp across the room as the muddy, red-paint-spattered, ragged mannequin was exposed to the crowd. Most of the room gazed in fascination, while the Five O's winced in embarrassment and fear. (All, of course, except for Derek, who was in a different school, but for the moment definitely in the Five O's.)

'Oh, jaypers,' Onion whispered.

'Please find herewith the evidence that has come to our attention,' The Ferg declared. 'Having been retrieved from the vicinity of the incident, it is believed by us, the gardaí, that this mannequin originally reside . . . residededed . . . lived! . . . originally lived at this address, specifically, the old hall at the back of this school.'

'This guy talks worse than Brody,' Onion whispered to Dallan.

'It's a type of English only spoken by guards,' Dallan told him. 'They have to do courses on it at garda college. I think it's meant to confuse eejit criminals into confessing.'

'Onion, don't you say a flippin' *word*,' Sive warned him quietly. 'Or I swear, I'll pull your tongue out of your head.'

'I wasn't going to say anything!' Onion hissed.

'Oh, *sure* you weren't. And don't let the teachers see your *eye* either. It's bouncing around like those balls on the lottery.'

'Do you think he knows anything?' Onion asked.

'Put it this way,' Sive replied. 'As long as we don't take any more chances for a while, I reckon we'll be okay. There's more than one dummy on that stage.'

'It is also alleged that this mannequin went missing some time on the Tuesday night,' The Ferg went on, 'but wasn't noticed missing until the Wednesday lunchtime, by the school caretaker, who uses it for practising his ballroom dancing. Furthermore,' he added, 'we believe that this prank may have been orchestrated by the Jackeen, as part of a major heist he's reported to be planning in the area.'

'We do *not* believe that bit, Fergus,' Judge sighed. 'That's just *you*. Flippin' hedgehogs, no wonder you keep failing your sergeant's exam.'

'So, I put it to you children . . .' The Ferg went on, ignoring his partner, 'were you or was . . . were . . . eh . . .'

'*Was*,' Judge growled.

' . . . Was anyone you know present at that loca . . . locat . . . at that PLACE on the evening in question? Do you have any information on the incident or those involved? If so, you can approach us directly or you can contact us on the confidential hotline. Your help would be greatly appreciated.'

There was a long silence once he'd finished. He waited, perhaps thinking that someone was just going to own up to the crime and he'd crack the case there and then.

'Is there a reward?' a girl asked.

It was Tina Dalton, standing near the back, working the angles as always.

An Appeal for Information

'What was that, little girl?' The Ferg responded. 'I don't follow.'

'Is there any *money* being offered for squealing on . . . eh, for *providing information*,' she said in a louder, slower voice, to make it easy for him to understand. Tina had little tolerance for idiots. 'Or do you just expect people to help the guards for free?'

'Well, uh, most people do,' The Ferg said in a weak voice.

Tina shook her head in dismay at the kinds of things 'most people' did. The sooner she was in charge of everything, the sooner the world would start making sense.

'Actually, there *is* a reward,' Garda Judge spoke up. 'Mayor Bump is offering five thousand euros for information leading to the arrest of the people responsible for wrecking his car – but you have to be an adult to claim the reward. Now, are there any further questions?'

Her tone suggested that there should *not* be any more questions, that she was done with this trivial, school-visiting, prank-investigation nonsense and there were proper criminals out there who deserved her attention. It suggested that the next kid to open their mouth was liable to be arrested for wasting a garda's time.

There were no further questions.

But the matter wasn't over, not by a long way. The Five O's all glanced nervously behind them, to where Tina was standing with the older kids. You couldn't say the words 'five thousand euros' in front of Tina Dalton without consequences. Because Ballinlud's Godmother of Crime would already be wondering why *someone else* was in possession of *her* five thousand euros.

Tina Dalton had taken an interest.

CHAPTER TWENTY: —
CLÍONA'S EXPERIMENT

Tina was not the only one who had taken an interest in the reward offered by Mayor Bump. In fact, half the school had decided it might be worth trying to solve the mystery. As they headed back to class, the four members of the Five O's had to listen to whispered conversations, questions and theories about who had stolen the mannequin and pulled off that disastrous prank.

'I almost wish we could tell them,' Dallan said quietly to the others. 'It was a brilliant piece of work.'

'Not a bleedin' word,' Sive said. 'It was a *flukey* bit of work and we were lucky to get out of there without getting caught. Let's just play it safe for a while. Especially considering who we've got for a teacher, right?'

Clíona had informed them of what she had seen the previous evening, and what Derek had told her, confirming Onion's suspicions that Mr Brody was, indeed, the Jackeen. Things had taken so many mad twists recently, the other two just gave in and accepted it. They had a dangerous, wanted criminal for a teacher. It was turning out to be one of those weeks.

For now, they had to sit in class and pretend everything was totally normal. The Jackeen was back in his Mr Brody suit, knocking objects over and continuing to sound like a blow-up bed as he walked around the room.

Onion's eye was being its usual, treacherous self, constantly turning to look in directions he didn't want, until Mr Brody couldn't help but notice.

'You there, boy. What's your name?'

'Onion O'Brien, sir.'

'What are you staring at?'

Clíona, who was sitting beside Onion, instinctively leaned away from him.

'I'm not staring, sir, I promise. I've got a wonky eye! It's like it's got a mind of its own sometimes. That's why I have the glasses and the eyepatch. I swear, I'm not staring!'

Brody stood over him, glaring down with a deeply suspicious expression behind the thick-rimmed glasses and the false moustache. Onion took a nervous breath of his inhaler and tried to look everywhere but at his teacher's face. His eye naturally did *exactly that*, as if challenging the master criminal teacher to a staring match. With shaking hands, Onion took off his glasses and the eyepatch so that Mr Brody could see both eyes. Onion was now seeing double. He could see two glaring Mr Brodys looming over him, twice as intimidating. He felt an urgent need to go to the toilet.

It was now clear to Mr Brody that Onion had a serious eye coordination issue. It seemed to be enough to lay his suspicions to rest for the moment. Seeing his teacher's body language ease off, Onion's nerves began to settle down slightly. Until he noticed that Clíona was holding a pin and appeared ready to use it. Clíona was about to carry out an *experiment*.

It should be pointed out that Clíona was something of a genius when it came to *things*, but could be a right eejit when it came to *people*, and her timing was never great.

Like now. Mr Brody turned away, and everything looked like it was going to be all

right. That is, until the next crisis. And Clíona reached out and fired up the next crisis right there and then.

She poked Mr Brody's backside with the pin.

There was a loud BANG, like a balloon popping, and half of Mr Brody's wide bottom suddenly went flat. He didn't react in pain, but in surprise, spinning around, a look of utter rage on his face. The class began to snigger. They just couldn't hold it in as they stared at Mr Brody's burst, floppy bum. Onion was sure that he and Clíona were about to be karate chopped to death by this deadly master criminal, when . . . when time seemed to stand still.

Onion could see everything happening in slow motion, as if he had all the time in the world to take it in. Everyone in the class had heard Mr Brody's bottom pop. Some of them had even seen Clíona stick the needle in. There could be no question that whatever happened next would be *bad*.

But what *could* happen next? If Mr Brody admitted that half his backside had just burst, then he'd be admitting that he was wearing an *inflatable* backside. And even if he could frighten the children in this class into silence, there would be questions – questions that would eventually seep through to the other teachers. This was a school: gossip spread like a tummy bug. Soon, everyone would be asking, 'Why did the new teacher have an inflatable bottom?', 'Why was he padded all over to make him look nearly twice as heavy as he was?'

Anything the Jackeen might do at this moment would make things much worse. He was here with a job to do and he needed to stay in character. He had to be a *teacher*, not anything else. Under no circumstances could he let it be known that he was a criminal in disguise.

The fury faded from his face. His body relaxed. Returning to his desk, he sat down – slightly lopsided – and stared at the surface of his desk for a few seconds, taking some deep breaths. Every child in the class gazed at him in fascination.

The sniggering turned into giggles and spread around the room.

WHEEEEEZZZ . . .

BAAAAAAAAARRRRRRRRP...

FIIIZZZ . . . HISSSSSSSSS

Brody's suit was now making all sorts of noises. The other children, all except the Five O's, thought they were coming out of his bottom.

'We shall do some history,' he said at last, switching on the interactive whiteboard. 'Let's talk about Vlad the Impaler, a Romanian prince who murdered tens of thousands of people by impaling them on stakes. If memory serves me right, I'm pretty sure he killed them all for laughing at him.'

The sniggering stopped and the class worked on in silence. The only noise that could be heard was Mr Brody's deflating suit.

CHAPTER TWENTY-ONE:
—
LIKE A SHARK'S EYES

'Why would you poke his bum with a pin?!' Sive asked Clíona as they walked out the school gate. 'Oh my God, have you lost your mind?'

'But we knew it was a padded suit. It wasn't going to hurt him,' Clíona said in a reasonable voice. 'I wanted to see if some of it was inflatable – and it was! Isn't that interesting?'

'"*Interesting*", she says,' Onion groaned. 'Interesting! Clíona, don't you get it? Now he knows that you know that he's not who he's pretending to be. And we're all friends with you. And he knows who we are! Our addresses are on the school computer. He can find out where we live! The guards have already come to the school twice, so he's got to be getting desperate.

'Whatever he's here to find, he hasn't found it yet. He's a cold-blooded, professional criminal and now he might think we're going to squeal on him. Imagine what he might to do to shut us up. What if he comes to our houses in the night to–'

'Onion, okay! Enough! Janey mack!' Dallan exclaimed. 'My head is melted enough as it is. Ease off with the Angel of Death stuff, will ya!'

But they all knew he had a point.

'I want my granny,' Onion said quietly.

'I think the only thing we can do, then,' Clíona told them, 'is to find what the Jackeen's looking for before he does. And I'm telling you, he's here for *Ned Belly's treasure*. We find it and hand it over to . . . I don't know, some of the grown-ups, and then he's got no reason to stick around, has he?'

The others weren't entirely convinced by this logic. Taking on the Jackeen at his own game seemed to be an excellent way to make things worse, and yet things were that bad already, the thought of searching for hidden treasure might help distract them from worrying about what the Jackeen had in store for them.

'But how are *we* going to find it if *he* can't?' Dallan asked. 'He's an expert at finding other people's money.'

'This is our turf,' Sive pointed out. 'We know every inch of this area. He's an outsider who doesn't know his way around. We need to do some research, to find out everything we can about the Ned Belly legend. The library's probably the best place to start.'

They all looked at Clíona.

'Say no more,' she said. 'I'm on it.'

'Do you think if we paid Tina for protection, she'd actually, like . . . protect us?' Onion asked.

'No,' the others all said immediately.

'Honestly,' Sive said. 'I think she'd just take our money and let us die. Besides, she might be dangerous for someone our age, but she is only *our age*. She's not in the Jackeen's league.'

'I don't know, though,' Dallan said. 'Give her time . . .'

There were mumbles of agreement on that one.

'Somebody talking about me?'

The voice sent chills through them. They turned around to find Tina standing behind them, flanked by the Bang-Off-Them Brothers. The twins had matching expressions, the vacant scowls of two empty minds waiting for instructions.

'So, what were you saying?' she asked again.

'We were just saying that you were probably going to win the talent competition,' Dallan replied quickly. 'On account of your being such an accomplished performer.'

'Damn right,' she said, sniffing. 'I'm curious, though. You lot are normally the first to get up to anything stupid that's going on. And yet . . . there's everyone else heading for the Valley, to see if they can find clues to who pulled that prank. They want to get that big reward, see? But not you. *You're* going in the opposite direction. I find that odd.'

'Yeah,' said Barry.

'Yeah,' said Larry. 'It's odd, that.'

'We've got other things to do,' Sive told her. 'What's your point?'

'Well, it's just that this *legendary* prank, which wrecked the *mayor's car*,' Tina went on, 'stinks of a bunch of people who are smart enough to set up something like that, and still stupid enough to create a mess of epic proportions. And it's weird how you're exactly the kind of fools who fit that profile.'

'There's *loads* of other fools who fit that profile!' Onion objected.

'That eejit eye of yours is wiggling,' Tina said, leaning in close so that her pretty face was only centimetres from his. She added in a soft voice, barely audible, 'Wiggle, wiggle, little eye. Wiggle, wiggle!'

Her own big, beautiful blue eyes were cold and dead, like a shark's, and her breath smelled of strawberries. Barry and Larry were tensing up, their fists clenched and knuckles cracked. They didn't like other people getting too close to their goddess.

'We're just heading down to the Valley now, to search for clues,' Onion said in a wobbly voice, nervously clearing his throat. 'To find out who did that thing. Isn't that right, guys?'

'Oh, absolutely,' Dallan said. 'We'll find out who did this. You just watch us.'

'That's *exactly* what I'll do,' she said, turning her cold gaze on him. 'I'll be watching you.'

And with that, she strode off, the twin brothers following along after her like the faithful dogs they were.

'Okay, things are getting out of control here,' Onion wheezed, leaning against the wall. 'My nerves can't take much more of this.'

CHAPTER TWENTY-TWO:
—
A RUN-IN WITH THE LAW

The gang felt like they needed some back-up, so they hung around the gate of Derek's secondary school, Ballinlud Community College, until the bell rang to mark the end of the school day and, more importantly, the beginning of the weekend. As primary-school children, they were considered an inferior breed by these older kids, to be tolerated, pitied, bullied, ignored or indulged, depending on the nature of the teenager involved.

Derek chose to try and ignore them. He was with a girl, Lauren Gaffney, and from the way they were talking, they weren't discussing schoolwork. Onion watched with a mixture of pride and sadness, imagining what it would be like to be the type of guy girls were attracted to. Onion just seemed to attract pity, scorn or mild amusement.

Lauren was tall, with bushy black hair firmly tied in a ponytail. She had a round, attractive face that laughed easily and wide brown eyes that were fixed on Derek. Derek had his cool face on, trying to pretend that he was being all casual, but Onion could tell his brother was all excited and nervous by the fact that he was tapping his phone against his thigh. It was a dead giveaway.

Derek had already seen the other Five O's and was trying to steer Lauren towards one of the other gates so that he could get out of the school without walking past his embarrassing younger brother. Onion trotted up to him, intercepting the couple as they came out onto the path outside the car park.

'Derek, we need your help!' he said. 'Clíona used a pin to pop Mr Brody's bum and now he knows we're onto him. And Tina Dalton's threatening us too! We think she knows about the whole . . .' Onion glanced at Lauren, '. . . that thing we did in that place we were talking about.'

'Not now, Onion,' Derek sighed, flashing an awkward grin at Lauren. 'I'll talk to you at home, yeah? I'm busy.'

'We can chat later if this is important,' Lauren said. 'Hiya, Onion!'

Onion blushed and stammered a greeting that came out somewhere between 'Hello' and 'Hi, Lauren' and ended up sounding like 'Hellauren,' which he thought might be an insult, and certainly earned him a scowl from Derek.

'Our teacher is the Jackeen!' Clíona announced, loud enough for some of the other teenagers to hear them too. Dallan put a hand to his face and Sive rolled her eyes. 'We think he's come to our school in disguise, because he's looking for Ned Belly's treasure.'

'Is that right?' Lauren asked, raising an eyebrow to Derek, who looked ready to punch Onion, and probably would have if there hadn't been witnesses.

'Don't mind them,' Derek muttered. 'They're just kids. They're always playing makey-uppy games.'

'The Jackeen's wearing a big, blow-up bodysuit as part of his disguise,' Clíona continued. 'I burst one of his buttocks with a pin. He's got half a flat bottom now.'

'*Has* he?' Lauren chuckled. 'Poor him!'

'Can you all just *stop talking*?' Derek growled at the Five O's. 'You sound mental.'

'No, I want to hear more!' Lauren said, folding her arms. 'So, he's after Ned Belly's treasure, is he? I suppose it's buried around the school somewhere? I heard that legend when I was little. About how the old hall, the one that was turned into a museum, was built on top of his grave, and there's a secret entrance down to his tomb.'

'We never heard that bit!' Sive exclaimed.

'Aw, Lauren,' Derek groaned. 'Don't encourage them.'

'Maybe that's why the Jackeen has been searching the old hall!' Onion said.

'My grandad worked in the museum when he was young,' Lauren told her. 'He looked all over it and never found anything. It's just a silly story for kids. That head still creeps me out, though.' She turned to Derek, smiling. 'I have to get going. Your friends here are *hilarious*, Derek . . .'

'They're *not* my friends. I'm not in their stupid gang.'

'Whatever. You should go help your brother investigate the Jackeen. It sounds like they've got a big mystery on their hands.' She gave him a big wink. 'Should be great craic! I'll catch you later.'

With a little toss of her head to the others as a goodbye, Lauren walked off towards the bus stop. Derek's jaw set in grim fury and he rounded on Onion.

'What is *wrong* with you?! Do you not know how *stupid* you sound? You made me look like an *idiot*! You can't talk about this stuff around my friends, okay? Flip's sake . . .'

'Tina Dalton thinks that maybe we did the prank in the Valley with the JCB,' Onion told him, hopping up and down in agitation. 'There's a reward out for catching the perpetrators and she'll figure out how to prove it was us sooner or later. And now, thanks to Clíona, the Jackeen knows that we're onto him. We have to find the treasure before he does, so we can sort all this out.'

'"Sort all this out"?' Derek snorted. He started walking towards home and the rest of them moved with him. 'Forget it, Onion. This has gone too far. We have to be realistic about this. This isn't the *Famous* bleedin' *Five*. We can't be messing with someone like the Jackeen. We need to take this to the guards. We've got enough on him. They only need to look at that office space of his to find out who he is. I say we call that confidential helpline and leave an anonymous tip.'

He took out his phone, switched it on, and then hesitated.

'What the . . .'

There was a new message on his phone. Derek went pale as he read it.

'What's wrong?' Onion asked. 'Derek? What is it?'

His big brother held the phone up so that the others could see. It read:

'*I know what you're doing. I know what you're talking about right now. I'm always watching. I can see you now, walking away from the school.*'

They all stared at the words. A shudder ran through every one of them.

'It was sent from my own phone number,' Derek hissed.

'Okay, that's really freaky,' Sive said in a tight voice. 'It's like he can see us right now.'

'He *can* see us right now,' Clíona told her. She pointed. 'Mr Brody's just across the road there, and he's staring straight at us.'

Onion let out a long, rattling breath, feeling his lungs flatten out like whoopee cushions as he and the others turned to see their teacher in his blue Ford Focus, parked on the far side of the road, his engine running. Mr Brody steered his car over to them, in no rush at all, and rolled down his window. He was smoking a cigarette, and he flicked some ash onto the strip of grass between the path and the road.

'Well, here we all are now,' he said. It wasn't his normal, flat, fancy voice. He had a thick Dublin accent. 'Isn't this a special moment, when we don't have to pretend anymore? When we can all be honest about what we are, eh? Not that anyone will believe you if yiz tell them who I am. Sure, you're only kids, aren't yiz? And I'm a respected teacher an' all that. Cheeky little move of yours, deflating my derrière like that, very impulsive indeed, *very* cheeky, if you excuse the pun.'

He blew out some smoke, then eyed them with a leering grin.

'I found some bubble wrap outside me door. When I stood on it I got the fright of me life. Now how did sheets of bubble wrap get to the top of me stairs unless someone brought it up there somehow? Proper little *Scooby Doo* bunch, ain't yiz? But this is the *real* world, children. And I'm not a pretend monster. I'm *the real thing*. A *proper* monster. And what's more, I was there when you little chancers stole that mannequin the guards are so interested in. That "accident" with the mayor's car, I'm sure you don't want anybody hearing about *that*, do yiz? I mean, maybe I should set the guards on yiz . . . or, maybe . . . I should deal with yiz *meself*, eh? Decisions, decisions . . .' He paused and smoked some more of his cigarette, blowing the smoke right at the children. 'So keep yizzer mouths shut and stay out of me way and nobody'll get hurt, all right? Are we all agreeable? Good. Off yiz go now. And don't forget to do all that quantum physics homework. Got to grow up nice and smart, don't yiz?

'That is,' he added, 'if yiz get to grow up at all.'

The window slid up again and he drove off, leaving five very frightened kids behind him.

CHAPTER TWENTY-THREE:
— THE OUTFIT

The Five O's shuffled towards home, each one lost in their own thoughts.

'What are we going to do?' Dallan asked.

'Go home and never speak of this again?' Onion suggested.

'Are we really gonna let this go?' Clíona asked. 'I'm fine with that, to be honest, but I just want to know that's what we're doing. He's a very scary man. I'm thinking that maybe bursting his bum was a mistake.'

'You're only thinking that *now*?' Onion snorted in amazement.

'He got in my phone,' Derek said in a shaky voice, gazing at the screen. 'He's *in my phone*.'

'I just wish we'd found the treasure,' Onion murmured. 'Maybe we could have used it to . . . I dunno . . . buy the Valley, and save it from those builders.'

'He had a book in his car,' Sive said at last. 'On the passenger seat. Did you see it?'

'A book?' Dallan repeated.

'Yeah. It was called *A Local History of Ballinlud*, or something like that. Did you not see it?'

'I saw that too,' Derek said. 'It's an old book about when Ballinlud was just a village and farmland, before it became part of Dublin. I've seen it before. Our history teacher has a copy.'

'Do you reckon the library would have a copy of it?' Dallan wondered aloud.

'They might,' Clíona said. 'Would the Jackeen kill us for going to the library? Or shop us in to the guards?'

Her question was met with silence. Nobody knew the answer. They were in uncharted territory here. A library visit could well prove fatal.

'We could pretend we're going for homework,' Sive said slowly. 'And not looking for treasure or trying to catch a criminal. Going to the library is, like, a totally normal thing to do, isn't it? People do it all the time.'

Again, nobody answered.

'I will go to the library,' Clíona said, with the tone of someone sacrificing themselves for a cause.

'I'll go with you,' Dallan told her, putting a hand on her shoulder. 'You shouldn't do it alone.'

'Are we really doing this?' Onion asked. 'Are we really going up against this nutter?'

'*Nobody* gets between me and the library,' Clíona replied firmly.

'How often do you get the chance to find hidden treasure?' Dallan said, shrugging.

'I'm doing it for the Valley,' Sive said, chewing her gum. 'It's our place. Maybe, just maybe, we can find this treasure and buy up the whole place and keep it forever.'

'Amen to that,' Dallan said, nodding.

'Derek?' Onion asked, looking to his brother.

Derek's face was a mask of stone.

'He got in my *phone*,' he snarled, brandishing the device. 'Like . . . like . . . right here in my *phone*. We're taking this turd down, Onion. And he's going down *hard*. Nobody messes with the *phone*!'

Onion stared at each friend in turn, hoping that one of them would ask him what *he* wanted to say. He wanted to stay safe and go home. He did not want to take on the dangerous criminal or risk going to prison for destroying the mayor's car. He wanted them all to back away from this and go on with living a normal life where they weren't risking their freedom or their lives on a trip to the library. And they were all staring back at him, waiting to hear what he had to say.

THE OUTFIT

He took a drag of his inhaler and swallowed a lump in his throat. His wonky eye wanted to look anywhere but straight ahead. These were his friends, his family. The Five O's. He would do anything for them. *Anything*. And besides, he had to admit that finding the treasure and buying the Valley for themselves sounded like a pretty cool deal.

'All right. Let's do this thing!' he said.

And they all gave big grins. They'd needed him to say yes. Onion wasn't the leader or the brains behind the Five O's, but he was the bit that held them altogether, as if the others were the bricks and he was the sloppy cement that got slapped in between them. He was the one who filled the gaps.

Clíona and Dallan started off towards town and the library. Onion, Sive and Derek would head back to the old hall later, to try and find the secret entrance Lauren had mentioned. If the Jackeen thought it was there, then maybe there was some truth to the old stories. It was still bright, though. They needed to wait until later, when they were sure Mr Oily Doyley would be gone home. In the meantime, they decided to gather some supplies back at the O'Briens' house.

As they walked, conversation turned to lighter matters – what everyone was going to perform for the talent show. Onion had already decided on doing some stand-up comedy. Sive wanted to do a hip-hop dance routine. Dallan had told them he was thinking about doing some magic tricks. Clíona hadn't mentioned anything, though she probably had some invention in mind and apparently she'd offered to help Youssef with his act.

Onion's eye narrowed just as they reached the back door. He stopped suddenly, blocking the others, and listened intently. He could hear the buzzing chatter of Granny's sewing machine.

'Oh no,' he whispered.

'Oh *yes*,' Derek said, laughing softly.

The costume. Granny was working on Onion's costume for the talent show. She was singing to herself.

Top 5 Things That Make Granny Happy

1. Singing to herself

2. A nice breeze out for the washing

3. A soft day, thank God

4. A good coddle

5. When Grandad stops talking

Granny was all *excited* about it. Sive went off to the shed to start gathering supplies while Onion, with a sinking heart, went into the back room next to the kitchen, where Granny Mary had all her sewing stuff out and was working feverishly away on some kind of deep-red, satin-like material.

'Onion, love!' she said in a delighted voice, as she caught him peeking in. 'You're just in time! Come on in. I've nearly got your outfit ready. I've only pinned it together for now, but you can try it on for size.'

Derek backed away from the door, his cheeks clenched to hide the smile on his face. Onion had no choice but to advance into the room and close the door behind him. Granny had made him a suit from scratch. She'd spent *hours* on it. He had a deep love for his granny and would hate to do anything to hurt her feelings. But he could see enough to know that this was going to be bad.

Taking off his uniform jumper, tie, shirt and trousers, he stood there in his undies while she assembled the outfit around him, some of it already sewn together, other bits of it held together with pins. He swivelled slowly round to face the mirror. Oh, dear lord, Onion thought. Oh dear lord, no . . .

THE OUTFIT

'Now, you look massive, son. Look at ye, ah just look at ye,' said Granny in a proud voice.

It was like something out of those tacky stage shows in the 1970s and '80s. He looked like an Irish Elvis Presley impersonator on his way to Las Vegas. The suit was *white*, with red satin bands up the collars and down the sides of the legs. The bottoms of the trousers flared out so wide they swayed back and forth like heavy bells and made 'whump' sounds as he moved. The shiny, red satin shirt had ruffles down the front and the collars looked big enough to serve as wings on a jet fighter. And there was a bow tie. He was wearing a big white bow tie.

'It's lovely, Granny,' he said quietly. 'But do you not think it's a bit . . . eh . . . a bit loud?'

'You don't dress down for the stage, pet,' she assured him. 'You have to be a *character*.' She spread her hands out above his head. 'You need a look that says "FUNNY".'

Onion took a deep breath and then nodded.

'You stay there, I want to show your grandad!' she said and hurried out of the room.

Onion was gazing miserably into the mirror when Derek came and nearly hurt his face laughing, having to hold a hand over his nose and mouth so that Granny didn't hear him. Tears streamed from his eyes, but even so, he came over and laid a hand on his brother's shoulder in sympathy. He had been the unhappy recipient of several of Granny's outfits over the years.

'I just want to go out there and say stuff that'll make people laugh,' Onion said, with a sniff.

'Onion, man . . .' Derek sighed weakly. 'You won't have to say a word.'

Grandad appeared in the doorway behind them, took one look at his grandson and swore under his breath. Then he called back into the hall:

'God almighty, Mary. You've made the boy look like a flippin' wedding cake with a dicky bow. Oh, and by the way, when you're finished with Onion's suit will you make us a pair of pyjamas? I've been sleeping in the nude since me old ones went missing!'

CHAPTER TWENTY-FOUR:
—
NEW INFORMATION COMES TO LIGHT

A visit to the library never felt so dangerous. Wherever they looked, Dallan and Clíona thought they saw the Jackeen watching, but every time, it turned out to be nothing. The Jackeen was a master of disguise, however. How could they be sure he wasn't watching their every move? They searched the local history shelves for the book but couldn't find what they were looking for, so they went up to one of the women at the desk and asked her. She was tall, well dressed and carefully made up, and looked friendly in a professional sort of way. She recognised Clíona, who was a regular visitor.

NEW INFORMATION COMES TO LIGHT

'*A Local History of Ballinlud*?' she said, tapping the desk with her long fingernails as she gazed at her screen. 'There's nothing here under that title, but I wonder could it be *Ballinlud: A Local History Collection*? Is it an old book?'

'Yes, I think so,' Clíona said. Derek had said it looked old.

'It's in our Local Studies section. In the archives, with all the other old materials,' the woman said. 'I'm afraid we don't normally allow children to handle them, Clíona. Even someone as careful as you. And you have to make an appointment with the head of Local Studies.'

The two Five O's hesitated. The longer they spent here, the more likely the Jackeen would catch them doing something he didn't like. And if they put in an official request for this book, there was every chance he might find out. If he could hack Derek's phone, who knew what else he could do?

Top 5 Ways You Can Be Tracked Without Knowing It

1. Your phone

2. Your phone

3. Bloodhounds

4. Aliens

5. Your phone

Clíona was about to say something to the librarian, then thought the better of it, and stood aside to let Dallan handle the situation.

'My good lady,' he began, leaning in, making sure his handsome features caught the beam of light shooting in the window across the desk. 'My learned friend Clíona and I are involved in a project for St Hilarius' National School, researching the history of Ballinlud, to be published in a bound collection of works by the pupils, which we intend to present to *Mayor Bump* on the opening of the new school classrooms. And . . . I'm sorry, what was your name . . .?'

'Catherine,' the woman replied.

'Lovely name . . . Well, as you know, *Catherine*, Mayor Bump is a *keen* enthusiast of local history, and I'm sure any assistance you could offer us would be properly credited in the bound volume, ensuring the *appreciation* of the mayor. It might well be reflected in next year's local authority budget. Every bit of *funding* helps, am I right, Catherine? I'd say it takes *lots of money* to keep stocked up on all these books. So perhaps

Clíona and I could take a *quick peek* at the book, and confirm that it contains the material we're looking for? It's for a good cause, after all.'

'Young man, that's an almighty load of guff,' Catherine said, 'but I commend you on your delivery. Mayor Bump better watch his back. You have a promising career in politics ahead of you. Okay, I know where the book should be, and you can have a look through it if you promise to be careful. We only have the one copy, so Clíona handles the pages. And you do it at the table there close to me.'

'It's a deal,' Dallan said.

The book was *very* old. It had been published in the 1970s, though some of the pictures in it were actually in colour. Dallan had always thought they had no colours back then. He let Clíona take the book and start leafing through the pages. Most of it looked very boring, with articles about the area's history, mostly about landowners and farming and a bit on the Industrial Revolution.

But there was a whole chapter on Ned Belly.

It was a history book, so it was more about the facts and details than it was about the interesting, horrible bits like Ned getting his head chopped off. But there was a map of the area. And the full rhyme was printed right there on the facing page.

'Look at this!' Clíona gasped. 'I searched all over the web for this and it was all here in an old book the whole time!'

'When Ned was dead, they took his head,
But no one listened when he said,
I'll die before you take my gold,
So keep back now 'cos you've been told,
The rise of spring in Ballinlud,
Will hide the place beneath its flood,
A dead man's fall, not hard to measure,
Still you'll never find my treasure,
I curse you all who'd steal what's mine,
You'll search and search and see no sign,

*The secret's lost with sly old Ned,
Hidden there on his dead head.'*

'There's two lines here that weren't in the last version,' Dallan noted, pointing. 'Look. The first one sounds like another instruction, doesn't it?'

*'A dead man's fall, not hard to measure,
Still you'll never find my treasure.'*

'What's a "dead man's fall"?' Clíona wondered. 'Is that, like, a body length? A body's length from what?'

She was staring at the map. It showed the stream and a few roads and paths, and there were fences or hedges around the edges of fields, and a lot more trees. There were hardly any houses marked. There wasn't even a church back then. It was all so different. Ned Belly's house was there though, close to a bend in the stream.

Dallan studied it now too, tilting his head this way and that as he tried to work out what part of Ballinlud the map showed. The Big Leak, marked as 'Diddle Stream', seemed to be about the same shape, but this was from hundreds of years ago. None of the modern roads or buildings were on it.

'That bit of road could be where Ballinlud Avenue runs now,' he said, putting his finger on one part of it. 'That's weird, the way the stream just stops halfway up, almost like it disappears. Maybe it went underground back then?'

'You can't really tell where any of these old bits would have been,' Clíona said, sounding disappointed. 'I thought we'd be able to use this to find the treasure.'

'But then *anybody* could have used it,' Dallan told her. He lowered his voice so that Catherine, the librarian, couldn't hear them. 'It couldn't be that obvious. I think the Jackeen's found something that nobody else has. Or at least, he *thinks* he has. That has to be why he's here now. And if there treasure's here, maybe he's got to find it before they build all the apartments on top of it.'

Clíona nodded. It made sense. She peered closer at the map. There was a word marked at the place where the stream seemed to disappear.

'I think it says "spring", but it's not clear,' she said. She turned the book around. 'Dallan, that's it! The stream's not disappearing *into* the ground, it's coming *out*! The Big Leak flows the other way, towards town. It's the spring, where the stream rises!'

They looked at each other, and then at the lines in the book.

'*The rise of spring in Ballinlud,*
Will hide the place beneath its flood.'

'I thought it meant spring, the *season*, but it's where the stream starts,' Clíona whispered.

NEW INFORMATION COMES TO LIGHT

'The treasure could be buried near the spring. Somewhere along the stream anyway, where it can flood.'

'But there's no real spring anymore,' Dallan said with a wince. 'The Big Leak comes out of a big pipe now, by the woods at the end of the school pitch. Everything would have changed when they were building the school and all the houses around here. The original spring could have been anywhere along where the stream is now.'

'We need to find something nearby that was there in Ned Belly's day and is still around now,' Clíona said. 'Then we can work out where everything else is and find the spring.'

They studied the map again. Dallan indicated another spot on the map. It was on land behind Ned Belly's house, close to where the spring was marked. It read simply, 'Well'.

'Hey. A well. Do you think . . . Could that be the Hole, do you think?'

Clíona looked up at him, her eyes wide. The Hole. That old stone chamber in the woods above the Valley, with the small hole in the top of it. The one that everyone dropped stones down to hear them fall into the water far below. It might once have been a well that had then been covered over with a stone lid. Only kids who played in the Valley knew about the Hole. But The Ferg had told them the Jackeen had grown up in Ballinlud. He had been a kid once.

Clíona took a ruler, some tracing paper and a pencil from her schoolbag. She traced the map and then guessed how far the Hole was from the stream in real life. That gave her a rough scale for the map, so she could work out other distances. Dallan went off to another part of the library and came back with a local guidebook that had a modern map of Ballinlud.

North was marked on the old map, so from the direction and distance she'd estimated, Clíona was able to work out where the original spring had once been. She put the ruler down on the modern map and lined the edge up in the right direction. It didn't lead to the big pipe at the bottom of the football pitch. The course of the stream had been changed, back when Ballinlud had filled up with housing estates.

The original spring had come up right where the old hall was now, in St Hilarius' National School. Clíona pulled her phone from her bag and took photos of the two maps and the text of the poem.

'The hall's being demolished after the talent competition,' Dallan said. 'If the Jackeen's going to find the treasure, he's got to do it soon.'

'Then so do we,' Clíona added.

CHAPTER TWENTY-FIVE:

EXTRACURRICULAR ACTIVITIES

Onion, Derek and Sive waited until well after dinner before setting out to do a thorough investigation of the old hall, and perhaps to find the hidden chamber Lauren had mentioned. Though they realised they were unlikely to find anything if others had searched the place long before them, they figured the Jackeen knew something that nobody else did or he wouldn't be bothering. He was a ruthless criminal. He had to be here for a reason. He had been searching the building the night before he'd shown up as a substitute teacher.

The hall, however, was already a hive of activity. Some of the teachers had stayed late to help get it ready for *Ballinlud's Got Talent*. The three kids were not entirely surprised to find the teachers there. They tended to believe that teachers had little else to do on a Friday night apart from getting ready for Monday morning.

Top 5 Things Pupils Think Teachers Do on Friday Night

1. Think about school

2. Go shopping for more boring clothes for school

3. Hoover the school

4. Play chasing in the school – they can run so fast with no pupils in the way

5. Talk to other teachers on the phone about other schools while drinking coffee

The three Five O's were about to turn around and leave their investigation until later, when Onion knocked on the open door and leaned in. Mrs Talcum was standing nearby, with a coil of colourful paper bunting in her hands, waiting to hand it to Mr Brody, who was standing up on a scaffold that had wheels on its base. He was taping more lengths of the stuff around the edges of the high ceiling.

Most of the hall stretched out to the left of the double doors, but there was a smaller room through another door to the right. This was where the new display case was situated, complete with motion sensors and cameras.

Ned Belly's head had not been put in there yet. They were saving that up for the day of the competition, and the valuable head was being kept in a safety deposit box in the bank until then.

Sive was frantically motioning Onion to back away from the double doors before he was spotted. He ignored her. This was better, he thought. With some of the other teachers here, Brody was unlikely to try anything nasty. This would be a chance to check out the hall in bright light and in relative safety. He considered this a major improvement on sneaking around and running the risk of bumping into the Jackeen in the dark.

Mrs Talcum was looking relaxed and a little flushed, as if she was actually enjoying herself. Some of the other teachers had the same look, like gardaí on holiday. The hall had been emptied out. There was a cargo container in the yard outside and most of the junk had been stored in it. The room looked completely different now, the floorboards swept of dust and the faded yellow walls cleaned of cobwebs. New lights were being rigged up. With the banners and bunting hanging up, the hall looked much brighter, and it was almost possible to imagine it as a proper venue for a big stage performance.

Tina Dalton and the Bang-Off-Them Brothers were there too, down the other end of the hall. The brothers were actually doing the work – sweeping the stage – while she supervised, helpfully pointing out bits that they'd missed. It was no great surprise to see her there. Tina was always careful to maintain her perfect image for the teachers. There was also a strong possibility she was here to figure out how she could cheat in the competition.

Onion stepped further into the room, catching Mrs Talcum's eye.

'Miss? We just came by to . . . eh . . . we . . . we left our football in the front yard. And we saw you all working in here. Do you need a hand?'

'Hello, Onion!' she said brightly. 'And Sive and Derek too! Yes, you could help if you like. Why don't you take over here, handing this up to Mr Brody, and I'll get on with wiring up the lights? Derek, Sive, you can start putting out the chairs. They're the folding ones, stored under the stage. It's all coming along well. We'll be able to put on a real show!'

Passing the coils of bunting to Onion, Mrs Talcum strode off towards the small room down the left-hand side of the stage, where the old piano was located, along with the fuse box and the hatch that led in under the stage. Sive and Derek were directed in there to pull out the stacks of folding chairs.

Brody looked down at Onion. Onion looked up at Brody.

'Come up here, lad,' the fake teacher said. 'And bring me that bunting. I need more of the pink ones.'

'I think I'll stay down here,' Onion called back, loud enough for others to hear. 'I'm not great with heights.'

'How are you with JCBs?' Brody asked, also speaking louder. 'I hear that digger flew up pretty high before it landed on the mayor's car.'

None of the other adults seemed to hear it, but Tina turned to look over, suddenly interested in the bunting team. Onion chewed his lip, and then started to climb up the ladder towards the master criminal.

'Be careful not to *fall*,' Brody said to him. 'We wouldn't want to lose you, now would we?'

He noticed that the Jackeen's bottom had been reinflated. The master of disguise must have patched it up. It looked normal once more. Climbing up close from underneath, Onion could see inside the bottom of the man's jacket. He could see the handles of tools held in loops around the inside of the jacket. That must have been where the wallet of lock-picks had fallen from. The Jackeen was making good use of all that padding. It was like a utility belt. He was fully tooled up for breaking and entering. But he still whizzed and hissed as he moved.

When he was standing up beside the 'teacher' in the bulky blow-up bodysuit, Onion checked around him, reassuring himself that he was in full view of all the *real* teachers. The ceiling of the hall was high, and the floor of the scaffold they were standing on was about four metres up. A fall from here probably wouldn't kill him. Someone who was naturally athletic might even escape unharmed. Onion would most likely fall in the most awkward way possible. Knowing his luck, he'd break his neck and his bum bone at the same time.

'What did I tell you about interfering, ya little guzzer?' Brody said softly.

'You said not to,' Onion replied, trying not to sound scared and failing completely. 'We're not interfering, honestly, we're just helping out the teachers.'

'Yeah, right. You expect me to believe that?'

'Why do you think I'm lying?' Onion asked. 'Is . . . is this where the treasure is? Is it in the hall somewhere?'

'Do you really think I'm going tell you that? What kind of eejit are you?'

Onion had actually been asked that last question many times in his life, and he still didn't have an answer for it. As far as he was aware, there wasn't any other eejit quite like him. At least, none that he'd ever met. Grandad always said he was 'the original article', which seemed unfair to Onion, who was sure there had been many other eejits before him. He couldn't have been the first.

He was about to respond when he looked down to see Clíona and Dallan walk into the hall. They spotted Onion up at a height with the Jackeen and their eyes went wide in shock. Onion glanced out across the rest of the room and, at that moment, noticed that nobody was looking their way except for the Five O's. The Jackeen noticed too.

With a flash of his hands, the master criminal seized the bundle of bunting from Onion's hands, whipped the coils over the boy's head, and shoved him over the railing, sending him plummeting towards the floor.

Onion barely had time to let out a wild squawk before he was pulled up short by a dozen different strings. He found himself dangling just above the floor, caught like a fly in a ridiculously happy-looking spider's web. The Jackeen had snared him in the bunting and caught him just in time. He lowered Onion to the floor. Mrs Talcum called over then, in a voice that was more tired and patient than annoyed:

'Onion O'Brien, will you ever stop fooling around! Let Tina take over. At least she has some sense about her. You go help with the chairs. Maybe you can manage to do that without getting tangled up in them?'

'Mind yourself, now,' Brody hissed at him from above. 'It's so easy to get *hurt* when you take on more than you can handle. And tell your friends. Steer clear until I'm done, or the next fall you take will be your last.'

But Onion's friends didn't need telling. The Five O's had all seen what had happened. His message had been received loud and clear.

CHAPTER TWENTY-SIX:
—
THE BIG NIGHT

Most of Saturday was spent rehearsing for the show that evening. The Five O's took turns keeping watch on the old hall, but there was no sign of the Jackeen making a move. They were all wondering what he was going to do, and whether or not he really knew where the treasure was. And what they would even do if he found it. During their sneaky exploration of the hall the previous evening, none of them had been able to find any sign of a secret doorway or hiding place.

At home, Onion kept practising his lines, over and over, and yet it wasn't coming together for him. He was a nervous wreck – even more scared than he'd been facing the almighty Jackeen. He was starting to think it wasn't worth it. He wasn't very popular in school and when he *did* make people laugh, it was normally by accident. Maybe this was a really bad idea. When he finally put on the outfit that Granny had made for him, and looked at himself in the mirror, he felt such a powerful fear rise up inside him that he nearly threw up.

This was a flippin' *terrible* idea.

Sive was first to arrive at the house, dressed in her hip-hop gear – baggy trousers, hoodie and trainers – all ready to throw down some moves. Despite her own nerves, she was in a much better mood, though she was chewing her gum at twice the normal speed. Dallan showed up then, in a tuxedo and a top hat, carrying his trunk of magic tricks. He was in his element, acting all smooth and practising his hand motions. There was no sign of Clíona. She wouldn't be performing. She was going to be too busy helping Youssef with his act, whatever it was.

'You lot ready?' Derek asked, poking his head in the door of the sitting room.

'No,' Onion said, trembling.

'Yes,' the others said, and dragged him out of the room with them.

Granny and Grandad joined the other kids' parents as they left their houses, everyone dressed in their best. It was a fine evening, and just about everyone was walking down to the school. There was a buzz in the air as people began to arrive into the hall. The performers had to wait in a line along the wall while everyone else took their seats.

A small entourage accompanied Mayor Bump into the hall. He held a glass box containing Ned Belly's head, and there was a big cheer as he took it in to the room next door, where it would be placed in its brand new display case, to remain there, open to the public, until the hall was demolished.

Then, he walked down past the crowd, waving and shaking hands and kissing babies, to take the seat reserved for him in the front row.

'Good luck,' Derek whispered to Onion, who was near the back of the line. 'Don't make an eejit of yourself. I'll stay at the back and keep an eye out for Brody, but I doubt he's going to try anything with everyone here.'

A chunk of space down at the end of the line, near the stage, was taken up by a piece of stage set, built to look like the prow of a ship. It was painted in black, with a white strip along the top, white railings, and *RMS Titanic* in black over the white strip. This was Tina's set. She was the only one to have such an elaborate setup. Larry Bang stood beside it. There was no sign of Barry. Tina would be last to perform.

Sive was first. She strode onto the stage as the music started and launched into her routine. She was good. She took her dancing seriously and the fact that her hearing was starting to fail had only increased her passion for music. But then something went wrong. At a key point, before she went for a jump, she got distracted and landed badly, twisting her ankle. She tried to keep going, but then something made her miss her timing again, and she stumbled over some quick steps she'd meant to take and tripped over. Getting up, she bravely finished her routine, but the life was gone from it. People clapped encouragement for her as she came off, close to tears.

'There was some scratching noise under my feet,' she told her friends, nearly snarling in frustration. 'It kept throwing me off. I think there's someone under there.'

The next contestant went up to do his bit. A kid doing keepie-uppies and other tricks with a football. He ended up messing it up too, looking down at the boards of the stage in annoyance. The performances went on, and the closer it got to his turn, the more nervous Onion became. He was shivering with tension. This was a really bad idea. *This was a really bad idea.*

There were other kids trying to look under the stage now. Several of them had been thrown off their routines by the sounds going on under there. The teachers and the audience couldn't hear them, only those who stood on the stage. The hatch at the side was blocked by the prow of Tina's *Titanic* and Larry was warning them to keep their hands off it if they knew what was good for them. *Nobody* was going to mess with

Tina's *Titanic*. Everyone was getting stressed out and it was making Onion all the more anxious.

Dallan went on and did his routine. He heard the scratching under the stage and didn't care. He just went right on with it. He was *loving* the attention. Onion looked on in awe as his friend did a series of well-executed magic tricks, ending with one where he took his top hat, covered it in a silk cloth, and then whipped the cloth away as the hat disappeared in an explosion of confetti. Onion's spirits sank further. He had nothing to compete with that.

Sive was now growling something at Larry and it was looking like a fight was about to break out over the stupid *Titanic*. The grown-ups were still watching the acts, but they were starting to get distracted too. Tina stood up and came over, dressed in a long, flowing white dress, an air of menace settling over that corner of the room as she laid down the law.

'What's going on here?' she demanded. The next person to touch her flippin' ship was going to need some serious first aid. Sive looked ready to take up that challenge. Things were getting a bit mad. Mrs Talcum was on her way over from the steps on the far side of the stage to see what was going on.

Onion closed his wonky eye. Stop thinking, he told himself. Stop thinking. He tried to clear his mind. Taking a blast of his inhaler, which hung on its cord over his red satin ruffled shirt, he held his breath . . . and then frowned. His heart, already pounding, quickened even more. What if the noise was the Jackeen? What if he was under there right now, digging away at the floor in search of the treasure? Was his big heist going down *right now*?

He was about to voice this thought to Dallan, who had come back up to stand beside him, when he was interrupted by the roar of an engine. Clíona had appeared. She shouldered her way past Sive, Tina and Larry and moved them back so that Youssef could get through.

Youssef was in his new wheelchair. As he rolled down past the crowd, his engine smoking heavily, his swimming goggles over his eyes, Clíona had climbed onto the stage and started pulling pieces of board from behind the curtains. Youssef tipped his wheelchair back and revved the engine. The machine scrambled up the six steps and onto the stage.

'Wow!' Onion said.

The engine was spouting a lot of smoke as Youssef did wheelies around the stage, and the first couple of rows of the audience were waving their hands in front of their faces and coughing. Some of them were looking on with concern as the kid in this homemade wheelchair started doing doughnuts, bunny hops and then short jumps off the ramps that Clíona had set up. Mrs Talcum came to the top of the steps, gesturing at Youssef to stop.

Unfortunately, nobody had checked the old boards of the stage to see if they could take this kind of punishment. Youssef's new wheelchair was substantially heavier than a normal one, and some of the floorboards had started to rot. Whatever the reason, as Youssef lined up for his final jump, with just barely enough stage to spare, Mrs Talcum came forward waving her hands and shaking her head, saying this was all getting too dangerous. Youssef fixed his goggles, grabbed his joystick and raced across the stage. He hit the ramp, launched himself into the air and came down at the end of the arc near the left of the stage.

He would have run out of room and probably flown off the stage, but he was saved by the fact that the boards gave way beneath him and the floor collapsed, sending him crashing into the space below. There was a scream of fright and Barry Bang came clambering out of the hole in the stage. There were howls of protest from the kids who'd had their routines ruined by the sounds beneath the stage. Clearly, Barry had been put there by Tina to throw everyone off their acts.

Barry looked around, badly shaken after the shock of having Youssef crash in on top of him, and then he turned and ran out of the hall.

There was a lot of shouting and laughing. Mrs Talcum called for order as some of the other teachers helped Youssef out of the hole. Neither he nor his high-powered wheelchair seemed damaged, and the audience were already calling for more. This was by far the most entertaining children's show they'd ever seen, and certainly beat the pants off the last nativity play they'd had to endure.

The hole in the stage floor was roped off with some cones and string. Mrs Talcum gave in to the pleas and agreed to carry on. She looked down at her call sheet, heaved a big sigh and then, speaking into the microphone, she announced:

'All right, next up, we have some comedy from . . . *Onion O'Brien*!'

CHAPTER TWENTY-SEVEN:
—
THINGS GET SERIOUS

As Onion approached the stage, he was shaking so much he could barely stand. He walked past Sive, who gave him a thumbs up, Tina, who gave him a death stare, Larry Bang, who thumped his fist into his palm, and then all the way down past the front row . . . all those adults, including the *mayor*, expecting to be entertained.

With the stage lights on, it was quite dark just off the edge of the stage. The steps were like an obstacle course for his clumsy feet. There were only six of them, but as he took the last one, he tripped, stumbled forward onto the stage, and his glasses slipped off his sweaty nose. They flew out in front of him and he managed to catch them before they hit the floor, only to straighten up and have his inhaler swing up on its cord and smack him in his wonky eye. He cried out, tried to put on his glasses, poked one of the arms into his good eye, cried out in pain again, and then turned to face the audience, his eyes askew. The audience got their first proper look at his outfit, with its red satin ruffled shirt, the white bow tie, the wing-sized shirt collars and the church-bell-sized flares.

As the pain in his watering eyes eased, he peered out from the spotlight and took in the room. They were in stitches laughing.

Just keep it coming, Onion, some part of his brain said.

'Well, I'm off to a great start,' he muttered into the microphone. Then, a little louder, he added, 'And you thought the biggest disaster tonight would be watching Tina Dalton sink on the *Titanic*.'

Some of the more nervous kids let out hysterical laughs, part amusement and part terror. Their high-pitched squeals made those around them laugh. The look on Tina's face would have sent a chill down the spine of an axe murderer.

'As you can see, I've got a wonky eye,' Onion continued, growing a little more confident, the shake fading from his voice. He pointed: 'It's *this* one, in case you were wondering. It has its advantages. There's not many who can have a staring contest with two different people at once. This thing gives me double vision though, which is pretty tough in school. It means I get twice as much maths homework as everyone else. And I can tell yiz, it's hard to count on your fingers when you keep seeing *twenty* of them.'

Most of the people were still laughing. Onion finally managed to get his glasses on without injuring himself. *Keep it coming*, that part of his brain was telling him.

'I was never any good at maths,' he said. 'I used to think an Algie Bra was a thing for measuring boobs.'

It was a stupid joke, but the grown-ups were all in a stupid mood now. One woman down the front had lost it completely. She had tears coming from her eyes. Onion had to hold back a smile. It was going to be okay . . .

Derek watched from the double doors near the back of the hall. Onion was being just enough of the right kind of eejit and he was doing all right. He felt an unfamiliar sense of pride in his brother. Of course, it helped that the audience were still giddy after watching a stuntman in a wheelchair crash through the floor onto one of the school bullies, but hey, you had to play to the advantages.

It was then that Derek heard the sounds coming from the room at the back, where Ned Belly's head had just been placed in its fancy new case. Warily, he walked towards the door into that room. Behind him, he heard the applause for his brother and then the final act was announced.

He paused, looking back to see Tina's *Titanic* set being manhandled onto the stage. Grandad and some of the dads had to pitch in, the thing was so heavy. Mrs Talcum nearly fell into the hole in the stage as she tried to direct the piece of set into position. A minute later, however, it was ready, and Tina took her position on the fake prow, with Larry crouched low behind her, holding the back of her flowing white dress, and waving it around to make it look as if it was blowing in the wind.

Derek opened the door into the back room and was surprised to find it empty. He was sure he'd heard someone in here. Then he noticed two things in quick succession: the one window, on his left, was open. And so was the display case. The Jackeen had got past the security cameras, the motion sensors and the alarms. The Head of Ned Belly was gone.

Derek's first reaction was surprise. Why would a master criminal bother stealing an old mummified head? Sure, it was valuable to Ballinlud because of its history, but it was hardly worth a lot of money, was it? He was after the treasure . . . wasn't he?

'It's been bothering me all day,' a voice said from behind him. He spun around to find Clíona standing behind him. 'The poem we found in the book? It was different to the ones we heard. And the last line was different.'

The secret's lost with sly old Ned,
Hidden there on *his dead head.*

'What do you mean?' Derek asked.

'The line says "on" his dead head, not "in" it,' Clíona repeated. 'I think there's some clue to the treasure on Ned Belly's head. Maybe a tattoo? And the Jackeen has to find the money soon, before all the building work covers it up.'

'He's only just stolen the head,' Derek said through gritted teeth. 'We can still catch him. I'm going after him. You go and tell everyone. I've had enough of this chancer. He's not getting away with this.'

'He's dangerous, Derek . . . !' Clíona called, but he was already running out the door.

Clíona rushed back into the hall. Onion, Sive and Dallan were walking down towards her. They'd spotted something was going on. She blurted out an explanation as they came up to her: Derek, Ned Belly's head, the Jackeen, the treasure.

Behind them, Tina Dalton was singing about how her heart would go on, but her eyes were on the kids at the back of the room who weren't entranced by her performance. They were talking in excited voices and distracting her audience.

Onion ran up onto the stage and grabbed the microphone. Tina wouldn't let go of it and continued to sing. Onion then screamed into the mic.

'Everyone, listen!' he shouted over the music. 'Everyone, the Head of Ned Belly has been stolen! It's the Jackeen! The Jackeen has stolen the head!'

Tina was still finishing her song as she tried to wrestle the mic from Onion.

Some people were laughing, thinking Onion was still cracking jokes, though they didn't get this one. People were talking now, asking questions. Mrs Talcum was calling on Onion to get off the stage.

Tina's voice faltered and then she stopped, looking out from her ship at the sea of puzzled, confused faces. It was over. Her chance at fame was lost, like the frozen body of a loved one sliding down under the sea. Behind her, Larry was still shaking the edge of her long dress, though the wind effect wasn't very convincing. She glared out across the audience at the three Five O's as they scurried out the double doors, shouting about the Jackeen.

'LARRY!' Tina roared at Larry. He hadn't even noticed Onion on the stage with Tina. He dropped the dress and ran towards him, just as

Onion dropped the microphone and ran off the stage.

'YOU'RE A DEAD MAN, ONION O'BRIEN!' she roared as Onion fled. 'YOU BETTER *KEEP* RUNNING, 'COS YOU'RE A DEAD MAN, YOU HEAR ME?!'

CHAPTER TWENTY-EIGHT:
—
THE CHASE IS ON

It was getting dark outside. Onion and the others ran outside and stopped, looking around. Sive pointed out across the football pitch. Derek was on his knees, his arms wrapped around his head. They sprinted over to him. When they reached him, he looked up at them, rubbing the side of his face. His eyes were glazed, as if he was stunned, and he was barely able to hold himself up.

'He's headed for the Valley,' he told them. 'The treasure's there, buried near the Hole.'

'How does he suddenly know where it is?' Onion asked. 'How do *you* know?'

'Because he found Ned Belly's map!' Derek said, holding up the head of Ned Belly. 'And then he bleedin' *hit* me with it when I caught up with him!'

'I wonder if that's the first time anyone's ever headbutted someone using someone else's head?' Onion said.

'Never mind that, *look*!' Derek snapped at him, thrusting the hairy lump of skull at him.

The Jackeen had shaved the top of Ned Belly's head. Under the hair, there was a map tattooed onto the scalp.

'Oh, that's gross!' Dallan said, gagging. 'I can't believe he shaved a dead man's head.'

'Ned's house is on here . . . and the stream . . . and the well,' Clíona said, taking the head from Derek. 'Look, there's an "X" marked near the well, on the stream side. Maybe five feet or so from it?'

'About the length of a body. A dead man's fall,' Dallan said quietly. 'Who gets a treasure map tattooed *on his own head*?'

'Someone who's a bit loo-lah,' Sive replied. 'Or has a twisted sense of humour. Like the kind of guy who'd spit in Oliver Cromwell's food.'

Onion was about to say something when a new sound cut him off. It was the noise of a powerful engine starting up. In the woods at the end of the pitch, they saw lights come on.

'The JCB,' Dallan said. 'He's got the JCB started! He's going to dig up the treasure right now!'

Nobody else was coming. People in the hall were still checking out the room, confirming the dead man's head had indeed been robbed while they'd watched the talent show. Everyone agreed that this was turning into quite the evening.

Onion wanted to go back to the grown-ups for help. Sive, Dallan and Clíona had already started running towards the woods. Derek was still on the ground, clutching his head and groaning. Onion gazed after his friends for a few seconds, seriously not wanting to mess with the Jackeen again . . . and then he started running too. He couldn't leave them to face this on their own.

Unfortunately, he was the slowest runner in the Five O's, his asthmatic lungs were starting to seize up with tension, and he was running in trousers that swung around his legs like flags. He was never going to catch up. He was ready to give up hope when he heard another engine, this one smaller, but much closer, coming up behind him. It was Youssef in his high-performance wheelchair.

'Hop on, Onion!' he called out. 'Let's go get this headnapper!'

Remembering how Clíona had ridden on the step on the back of the wheelchair, Onion jumped on. Youssef pulled down his swimming goggles and opened up the throttle. They reached the edge of the woods a minute later and started down the widest path, the heavy-duty wheels bumping and thumping over the rough ground, making it hard to hang on as they bounced along. The wheelchair had a small LED headlight and Youssef switched it on.

They burst out into the end of the Valley in time to see the Jackeen working the JCB's backhoe, the big mechanical shovel on the back of the digger. He had got rid of his bodysuit, glasses and moustache and was dressed in dark, figure-hugging clothes. In the beams of the digger's bright work lights, the shovel had already made a hole beside the well and pushed a large, flat stone aside. Now the mighty arm dug a small, badly rusted iron chest up out of the ground. Tucking the shovel up so that it held onto the chest, the Jackeen turned his seat forward to face the steering wheel and put the JCB in gear.

This was where things started to go badly wrong for everyone concerned.

Sive, Dallan and Clíona had been sneaking up behind the Jackeen, which meant that they were *in front of the digger* as he went to drive off. He hesitated for a moment, scowling at the three children blocking his way. Then he grinned horribly, shoved forward a lever to lower the front shovel and drove straight towards them, as if to run them over like a bulldozer. Instead, the shovel scooped them up and raised them high into the air as the JCB turned towards the gap in the bank that led out onto the road.

'Always nice to have some *hostages*!' the Jackeen shouted through the open side window. 'Hang on tight now, I wouldn't want to drop any of you!'

He cackled and swung the wheel, swerving left onto the main road, accelerating as he headed up the hill towards the school. Youssef was already racing after him, with Onion hanging on the back, being rattled to the bone by the jolting motion of the revved-up wheelchair. His white suit was getting spattered with mud and dust and his flares were at risk of catching on the chunky motorbike tyres. He looked a right twit. He wanted to tear off the bow tie that was constricting his throat, but he didn't dare take a hand off the handles on the back of the chair, for fear he'd be thrown off.

'When I get you close enough,' Youssef called to him, 'you can jump on and tackle him, okay?'

'I can . . . wait . . . what?!' Onion screamed back.

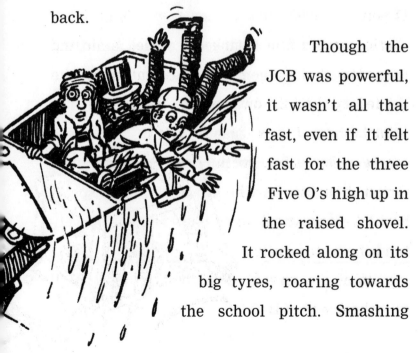

Though the JCB was powerful, it wasn't all that fast, even if it felt fast for the three Five O's high up in the raised shovel. It rocked along on its big tyres, roaring towards the school pitch. Smashing through the wide wooden gate, the Jackeen kept a straight line across the football pitch, child hostages in the front shovel and treasure chest in the back. He was heading for the far end, trying to make his escape.

'Oh my God, this is insane!' Sive yelled.

Even as she said it, they were passing the end of the school car park. A garda car came through on screeching tyres, bumping up onto the grass and speeding across towards them. It was The Ferg and Garda Judge. They were going to try and cut them off. The Jackeen cackled again and turned in towards them, the digger smashing into the front of the car and sending it spinning. The Ford Mondeo was no match for a JCB. Youssef, however, was still in hot pursuit. The lawnmower engine seemed to have found an extra bit of speed, now that it was back in its natural home of well-tended grass.

'Hang on, Onion,' Youssef shouted. 'We'll only get one shot at this!'

'One shot at *what*?!' Onion shrieked. 'Youssef, don't–!'

But it was too late. Youssef was already doing his thing. He overtook the JCB, swerved suddenly sideways and hit the brakes hard.

'JUMP!'

Onion's reflexes obeyed even when his brain tried not to. The wheelchair jerked forward and he leapt, the jolt of the step under his feet acting like a springboard. He was hurled into the air, arms and legs swinging wildly, and slapped against the glass of the side window. The Jackeen was taken by surprise, seeing a red-headed, wonky-eyed child in a tacky, white, 1970s flared suit, his spindly body flattened against the glass. The master thief jerked the steering wheel, the JCB swung around and the front of it plunged into an expensive-looking Mercedes at the end of the car park.

The impact jolted Onion again. He came unstuck from the glass and was thrown onto the grass below. The Jackeen tried to reverse away from the car he'd just crushed, but the front wheels were all caught up in the wreckage.

He cursed at the top of his voice, opened the door and jumped from the cab, only to find himself facing The Ferg.

'You're in trouble now,' the burly garda said.

The Jackeen looked around just as he was caught by a spinning kick from Garda Judge that nearly took his head off. He dropped to the ground unconscious, and that was that.

The audience of the talent show were flooding out into the car park now, to see what all the fuss was about side. Seeing the wrecked Mercedes, Mayor Bump roared in outrage:

'I don't believe it! *I don't believe it*! THAT'S MY CAR! AGAIN!'

CHAPTER TWENTY-NINE:
—
THE FATE OF THE VALLEY

A s more guards arrived to help secure the scene, people congratulated The Ferg and Garda Judge on their capture of the famous criminal and the rescue of these unfortunate children. There was a distinct lack of surprise, particularly among the teachers, that the Five O's had been involved in this dramatic chase. It was exactly the kind of spectacular misfortune that the four children normally got caught up in.

Derek had fully recovered from being headbutted with Ned Belly's skull. He was smiling at the whole scene as he helped his bedraggled brother back onto his feet. Sive, Dallan and Clíona were paying little attention to the guards who had 'rescued' them, and were standing around Youssef instead, slapping him on the back and shaking his hand.

The mayor was standing over his brand new car, crying as one of his aides rubbed his back to comfort him.

'And what *exactly* has been going on here?' Mrs Talcum asked Onion and Derek, as the guards focussed their attention on the stunned Jackeen.

'We were trying to find Ned Belly's treasure, Miss,' Onion said, still feeling a bit dazed. 'We wanted to save the Valley. But the Jackeen figured out the map to the treasure was on Ned Belly's head. He dug up the treasure and was going to do a runner with it.'

He pointed to the mummified head Derek had tucked under his arm, and then to the iron chest, still held in the JCB's backhoe. Mrs Talcum took the head from Derek and studied the map, then walked over to the digger to examine the iron chest. The bumpy ride in the shovel had split open the rusted iron lid, and gold glinted inside. The other Five O's and Youssef had come over now to have a closer look. Other people were starting to notice the iron trunk too, including Mayor Bump.

It looked like a message was scratched into the underside of the lid. Onion peered closer, trying to focus his wonky eye on the words. He read the ancient message aloud:

'Cromwell is a cad.'

'Must be Ned Belly's idea of a joke,' said Derek. 'He's almost as rubbish at comedy as you, Onion.'

'This gold has historical significance,' Mrs Talcum said. 'The Jackeen can't claim it, especially as he's broken the law to find it, and because it's an archaeological find. It probably belongs to the State.'

Onion felt a massive, sinking disappointment. After everything that had happened, they had still failed to save the Valley.

'However,' the teacher continued, holding up Ned Belly's head, 'if this map really does show the site of Ned Belly's *house*, and the fact that it also marked the treasure seems to prove it, then the Valley has to be considered an area of historical significance.'

'No,' Bump said, holding his hands up. 'No, now hang on . . .'

'All work will have to stop until they've done a survey of the site,' Mrs Talcum added. 'And I expect there'll have to be an excavation to examine any ruins. I'd say the building work could be held up for months or years.' She winked at the Five O's. 'Maybe forever.'

The kids began jumping around and cheering, high-fiving and chanting.

'THE DIGGER IS RUBBISH! THE BUILDER IS BAAAAAD! SAVE THE BIG LEAK! WOOOOO AAAAAGH!'

The chant didn't really work this time as there were no builders about, but it didn't matter. The Five O's had saved the Valley and the Big Leak . . . at least for now.

'No, no, no, . . .' Bump was saying, but he had a hand to his face. This was a man having a very bad day.

Not as bad as the Jackeen's day, however. He was being led away in handcuffs, bearing a blossoming black eye, with a circle of guards around him. The Ferg was glowing like a light. Garda Judge stood back, watching with her arms folded, showing just a hint of satisfaction at a job well done.

Granny and Grandad were on their way over, and Onion groaned at the fuss he knew Granny was going to make over his ruined outfit. Derek chuckled, looking at the state of his brother. Then he saw Tina off in the distance, in her long white dress, coming towards them, an image of cold fury, silhouetted against the lights of the hall like a shard of ice in the lights of a sinking *Titanic*.

'Oh, that reminds me,' Derek grunted. 'I wonder who won the talent competition.'